Badgerman and Bogwit...

Since leaving N... has been
a teacher a... e is now
involved in ... enever
he has the ... ounty
similar to the ... is set.
His first two ... and *Roosters*, are
also published ... ...aber.

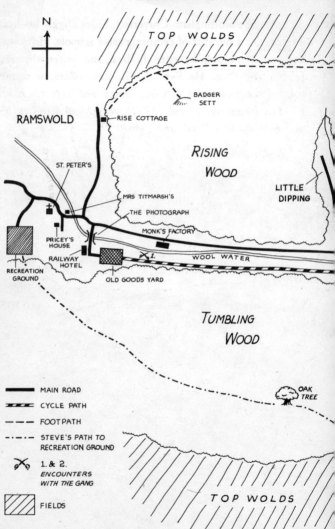

BADGERMAN & BOGWITC

N

TOP WOLDS

RAMSWOLD

RISE COTTAGE

BADGER
SETT

RISING
WOOD

ST. PETER'S

MRS TITMARSH'S

THE PHOTOGRAPH

LITTLE
DIPPING

MONK'S FACTORY

PRICEY'S
HOUSE

RAILWAY
HOTEL

WOOL WATER

1.

RECREATION
GROUND

OLD GOODS YARD

TUMBLING
WOOD

MAIN ROAD

CYCLE PATH

FOOTPATH

STEVE'S PATH TO
RECREATION GROUND

OAK
TREE

1. & 2.
ENCOUNTERS
WITH THE GANG

FIELDS

TOP WOLDS

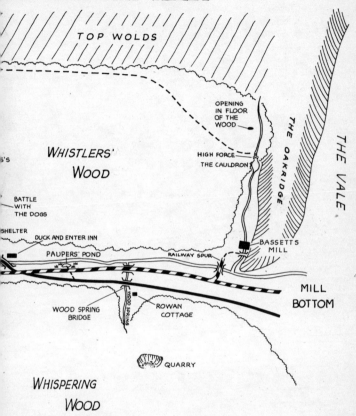

THE RAMSWOLD VALLEY

TOP WOLDS

WHISTLERS' WOOD

OPENING IN FLOOR OF THE WOOD

HIGH FORCE
THE CAULDRON

THE OAKRIDGE

THE VALE

'S'S

BATTLE WITH THE DOGS

SHELTER

DUCK AND ENTER INN

PAUPERS' POND

RAILWAY SPUR

BASSETTS MILL

MILL BOTTOM

WOOD SPRING BRIDGE

WOOD SPRING

ROWAN COTTAGE

QUARRY

WHISPERING WOOD

FARM

TOP WOLDS

by the same author

INSIDE THE GLASSHOUSE
ROOSTERS

Badgerman
and Bogwitch

GILES DIGGLE

faber and faber
LONDON · BOSTON

First published in Great Britain in 1993
by Faber and Faber Limited
3 Queen Square London WCIN 3AU
This paperback edition first published in 1994

Printed in England by Clays Ltd, St Ives plc

A CIP record for this book is available
from the British Library

ISBN 0-571-17165-6

2 4 6 8 10 9 7 5 3 1

For Ann

Acknowledgement

With thanks to Louisa Sladen who edited the various versions of the book with tact and sensitivity to the needs of the story.

Stephen Armstrong lay on his bed in the attic bedroom trying to tune the radio. He was irritable. The window in the gable end of the room was open and so was the skylight, but it was still stifling hot under the eaves. The evening was airless. There had been no breeze all that day. The summer solstice was living up to its reputation for being a long-drawn-out affair. Even now the roofs of Ramswold burned like kitchen coppers in the light of the sinking sun.

Steve gave up on the radio and pressed it face down in the duvet. He propped himself up on his elbow and stared sullenly at his brother's suitcase on the bed beneath the window. When his shoulder began to hurt he rolled over on to his back. He couldn't get comfortable. Nor could he get the repeated refrain of the girls in the street out of his head. Why were they so happy? Why didn't their parents call them in to bed? Why didn't they just belt up? Round and round the skipping rope clicked, just as it had ever since he'd come up to his room. It was a stupid, useless pastime.

> Bogwitch, Bogwitch
> tricked a toad,
> turned three times
> and touched her toes.

On and on it went, relentless and nonsensical, each refrain followed by another, identical to the first but for the third word changed to another like *teased* or *tagged* or *tacked* until the substitutions disintegrated into giggles, a new person skipped into the middle and the whole thing went round again. Where did they get their energy from, these girls?

Shut up, why didn't they? Couldn't they see he wasn't in the mood?

Then the kitchen door slammed two floors below. Richard was back. Where had he been? He was an hour late.

Richard wasn't even coming up to see him. Instead he was putting a solitary tea-bag in a mug for himself. How selfish! He never used to be like that before he left school nearly a year ago.

The small attic room was too cramped for them now that Richard had grown into a man's body and Steve, at fourteen, was following apace. Richard had been keeping odd hours, arriving home after midnight and sleeping late at weekends. Steve found these interruptions to his regular patterns of sleep exasperating. Borrowing his bike was the last straw. And why had he given in to his brother's demand? He was too easy going, that's why. No, that was a lie. He was scared of getting another bone-deep bruise on his arm. That was the real reason why he had agreed, and he hated Richard for making him feel that way.

Why couldn't his brother walk into town like other people did? Why did Richard assume that when his motorbike was off the road he could just take the bike whenever he wanted? He couldn't accept his younger brother having anything new, that was why. Steve should have been glad that Richard was leaving home, but he wasn't. It changed everything.

'Where've you been?' asked Steve, bursting into the kitchen, his voice breaking into an unfortunate squeak just when he'd hoped to take the offensive.

Richard kept his back to him, painstakingly stirring the

tea-bag around in his mug. The teaspoon clinked nervously against the thick porcelain. His hand was shaking. He said nothing in reply to his brother's question.

'I was supposed to meet Pricey half an hour ago for the photograph,' Steve continued sullenly. 'I should have walked down.'

But he couldn't have. He had been scared to leave the house in case his brother came back and moved out without saying goodbye.

'He'll wait,' said Richard.

'He can't. It has to be done at six twenty-one precisely, in the same spot, whatever the weather. We've done it every year since he asked for that stupid camera for his seventh birthday.'

'Well, you can do it a bit later, can't you? What's all the fuss about?'

'It's not the same,' Steve protested. 'It means that things have changed. Everything will be different.'

'You're stupid!' said Richard, refusing to turn from the draining board, where he leant on his elbows sipping his tea. 'You and your bloody superstitions. It's about time you grew up!'

Richard had to have the last word. He could never understand how important it was for Steve to adhere to the small rituals which ordered his life and added to the pleasure of experience. Richard had always been a parcel ripper, whereas Steve had always opened Christmas presents according to a set pattern: smallest and lightest first, working towards the biggest and finally the heaviest. Each one had to be set down on the floor with an appropriate space in between. They had to be turned over carefully, one after the other. Every parcel had to be gently shaken and listened to. By the time Steve had begun on the first, Richard had torn the paper from his last. Then Steve would have to elbow him away. 'Meanness' was Richard's name for it; Steve called it 'care'. It was bad luck to tear the paper in the unfolding. Richard never could understand any of that.

For the past seven years Steve had gone with Pricey on his birthday to pose for a photograph on the bridge in the centre of Ramswold. Each year they appeared older, invariably smiling, but never any the wiser as to why they put so much store by the ceremony. Now the chain had been broken. The years and their childhood were slipping away and it made Steve feel uneasy. Richard had spoiled everything.

Unable to get through to his brother, Steve said: 'I'm going.' Then, ashamed with himself for giving up the argument so easily, he added: 'You'd better not have damaged it!' Since he had been given the mountain bike at Christmas he had steadfastly refused to go anywhere without it.

Richard shrugged himself off his elbows and tossed his mug into the sink amongst the dirty dinner plates for his mother to sort out later.

'Go stuff yourself, Steve!' he said, and stomped angrily past his brother towards the stairs.

Steve began to follow but thought better of it, and crossed the tiny kitchen to the back door. They called it the back door, but it was in fact the only way in and out of the house – a small, two-bedroomed stone cottage nestling against a bank at the top end of Ramswold beneath the dark trees of Rising Wood. It had been Steve's home since his birth. He had always loved it, but for the first time, last winter, Rise Cottage had seemed cold and cramped, a world away from the cosy warmth of his childhood. He neither understood nor liked the change.

Down the street, a door opened.

'Janet!' a male voice called.

The skipping song faltered to a stop and the rope fell limp. The sun slanted down into the yard, picking out the red of his mother's potted geraniums and the gaudy pinks and blues of the hanging baskets crammed with lobelia and petunias. The marigolds in the window box were desperate for water. Richard's motorcycle rusted in one corner above a pool of oil. The dustbin stank familiarly of ash and potato peelings. But something was missing. His bicycle was gone.

Steve flung open the gate and dashed into the street. His mother and father were struggling up the hill with the weekend's shopping, but instead of going down the road to lend a hand, he dashed round to one side of the house and then the other.

By the time he returned to the gate, his parents were almost upon him.

'Steve, give your mother a hand, you lazy tyke!' called Mr Armstrong.

But Steve had shot in through the gate without waiting to listen. He slammed open the kitchen door and flew up the narrow staircase two steps at a time.

Richard was lying on the bed, grimly holding back humiliating tears of rage.

'Where's my bloody bike?' Steve screamed, picking up his pillow and hurling it at Richard.

Steve expected a fight, but his brother offered no resistance.

'I said, where's my bike? What have you done with it?'

'Been nicked', said Richard, rolling over to face the wall.

'What do you mean?' Steve shouted, grabbing his brother roughly by the shoulder.

'Hey! Mind my shirt! You'll tear it. I only bought it last week.'

'Where's my bike?' Steve persisted, screwing the

shoulder of the shirt into a tight knot. Richard attempted to pull away and as he did so the seam came apart at the neck.

'Little bastard! Look what you've done now!'

Richard twisted round and jabbed his fist into Steve's stomach, but Steve hung on. Then there was another ear-splitting tear as the two brothers toppled on to the floor.

'Stop it! Stop it at once, do you hear!' shouted Mrs Armstrong as she clattered up the stairs. 'Can't we leave you boys on your own for five minutes without you breaking the house apart?'

Then Mr Armstrong was there too. He didn't bother wasting words. He grabbed one fistful of hair in each calloused hand and pulled his sons apart. Richard lashed out at his father, only to find himself hurled on to the bed like a sack of old washing.

'Now cut it out, both of you! I want you down in the kitchen, this minute. We'll sort this out over a cup of tea. Steve, you get the kettle on and calm down. Richard, you can start the washing up while you think what to say!'

Once downstairs, Mrs Armstrong sat tensely at the kitchen table and communicated silently with her husband who stood against the cooker, grim faced, with his arms folded across his chest. Mr Armstrong was balding and his hair greying, but he had lost none of his vigour since being laid off from the piano factory after it burned down. He was used to being in full possession of his sons and he didn't take kindly to being messed about.

Mrs Armstrong feared an over-reaction. The fight was just one more thing to cope with, and she wanted the matter done with as quickly as possible. Nevertheless, she would back her husband in front of her sons, however much she might argue the case in the privacy of their bedroom.

'So? What's this all about then?' asked Mr Armstrong.

Both boys opened their mouths to speak.

'You first, Steve.'

'He's lost my bike!' said Steve, trying not to spill the tea as he set the cups down on the table.

'What do you mean?' asked Mrs Armstrong, sensing that things were worse than she imagined.

'My bike's been stolen. The idiot's borrowed it and lost it.'

'How and where?' asked Mr Armstrong, rounding sharply on his elder son. 'And what were you doing with it in the first place? I've spoken to you before about touching that bike.'

'I needed to get some spares. The garage shuts at five-thirty.'

'You should get organized, Richard,' said Mrs Armstrong. 'You stayed in bed all morning and lazed around all afternoon.'

'Well, I work all week, I need to take it easy on Saturdays.'

Richard had said the wrong thing and he knew it. His mother flew at him.

'Your father has worked hard all his life, and you'll never catch him lazing in bed all day, not even now, and God knows he's got more reason to than most!'

'Leave it, Sally,' said Mr Armstrong quietly. He composed himself, and then continued. 'Well, young man, what exactly did happen?'

'I only popped in for a minute. I left the bike round the side of the workshop and when I came out it was gone.'

'Couldn't even be bothered to lock it up, I suppose,' said Steve.

'How could I? You didn't give me the bloody key!'

'Less of the language, do you hear?' snapped Mr Armstrong.

'Yes, sorry,' muttered Richard.

'Steve, I know you're upset and angry, but you're not helping the situation.'

'But what about my bike?' protested Steve. 'And how am I going to get to school on Monday?'

'It was insured, wasn't it, Rob?' asked Mrs Armstrong.

'No,' said Steve, bitterly, 'we never got round to that!'

'I'm sorry, Steve,' said his father, putting his arm around his shoulder, 'but there's not a lot we can do about that now.'

'Oh, Rob!' said Mrs Armstrong.

'Don't start that, Sally, please! You know how tight things have been.'

'Even so,' she protested. 'It was short-sighted.'

Mr Armstrong bit his tongue. The mountain bike had cost him more than he could afford, and if it hadn't been purchased at cost price through his old school-friend, Malcolm Monk, it wouldn't have been bought at all. Monk's hand-built bikes didn't come cheap. But it wasn't the time for arguing with his wife and for that, at least, Steve was grateful. There had been too many squabbles recently.

'I'm afraid, Steve,' said Mr Armstrong, turning to glare at his elder son, 'you'll have to wait until Richard can pay you what he owes you for the bike. Until I get back to work, there's no money. There's barely enough from what your mum earns to pay the bills. Otherwise we'd see you right.'

'I'm not paying,' Richard protested, 'It wasn't my fault it got nicked!'

'Then whose fault was it?' asked Mrs Armstrong, her voice rising angrily. She hoped she hadn't brought up her son to have that kind of attitude. The Armstrongs paid their way, they always had.

'I don't know,' said Richard, 'but I'm not paying. I can't afford to. I've had to hand over half of what I earn to you already, and that's been bad enough!'

8

'Why, you ungrateful little sod!' Mr Armstrong's temper flared. 'Get out! Get out before I do something your mother will never forgive me for! Get out! And don't come back until you've got something to say for yourself!'

'Rob, don't,' said Mrs Armstrong quietly, but it was no use.

'Don't worry,' Richard screamed, 'I've already packed. I'm going!'

Steve chased after him.

'You'll soon find out how much living actually costs,' shouted Mr Armstrong.

'Rich, wait!' Steve pleaded. 'Don't be stupid!'

His brother ignored him and shrugged him off when he tried to grab his arm at the foot of the stairs.

'Rich!'

'Sod off, Steve, I've had enough of all of you!'

With that, Richard fetched his bag and stalked out of the cottage. He had planned to leave later that evening anyway. Although the Armstrongs were unhappy about him moving in with the squatters at the Railway Hotel, they had hoped to put on a brave face and send him off with a smile. Instead, his going was more acrimonious than any of them could have expected.

Steve followed his brother for a few yards down the hill, but then gave up.

'Idiot!' he cursed. Why did they have to row? Why couldn't they just sit down and talk about it?

When Richard was out of sight, he set off in search of Pricey.

If there was anything that could have brought some cheer to Stephen Armstrong on that miserable evening in June it should have been Ramswold. He had lived there all his life and its joyful familiarity had never before failed to raise his spirits. Situated at one end of a narrow wooded valley, the town was so in harmony with the landscape that its buildings might have sprung up straight from the earth.

The streets were narrow and many of them cobbled. Ramswold was full of twists and turns, humps and bumps and hidden corners. It was a test to the fit and a trial to the elderly, but everyone managed to find their way around somehow.

Ramswold had always been a delight to the eye and the ear. Cascades of water burst unexpectedly through walls, frothed over troughs and rushed down gullies and stone-lined conduits, only to disappear just as suddenly through other walls or down mysterious drains. 'All's well in Ramswold, all's well in the world!' Mr Armstrong had assured his sons before he closed the bedroom door on every evening of their childhood. But all was no longer well in Ramswold. Litter dammed the gutters and choked the drains. There were thefts and factory closures, drunkenness in the streets at night and now conflict at home. That evening, Ramswold wore a rather forlorn look, and the drought-stricken streams could barely gurgle. The air was yellow, tinged with dust.

Steve found Pricey labouring up the hill towards him. He was a fine musician, a miracle on the piano and a master of the saxophone, but an athlete he was not. Pricey was pushing his dad's ancient fold-away bike and couldn't have made harder work of it had he been pushing a pram-load of coal. Pricey could get a sound out of almost anything given five minutes to practice, but at the moment the only noise he could produce was an unpleasant rasp.

'Where've you been?' he gasped, as Steve drew near. 'I waited ages!'

'Why didn't you come up?'

'Why didn't you come down? That was the arrangement.'

Seeing that Pricey was irritable from the unwelcome

10

climb, Steve stopped being annoyed. Pricey, for all his faults, was his best friend.

'My flaming brother got my bike stolen.'

'What? Your new bike? How?'

'His usual carelessness. My dad's told him never to come back home again.'

'Really?' said Pricey, but Steve wouldn't go into details. Even though Pricey was a good friend, Steve usually kept domestic problems to himself.

'Well, we've blown the photograph, haven't we?' said Steve, as Pricey turned the bike around.

Pricey fiddled awkwardly with his brakes. 'This cable's really slack,' he said, hoping to divert Steve into a discussion of bicycle mechanics.

'Pricey,' said Steve, 'don't be pathetic. Even you can see that these brakes are in perfect working order. You might as well confess and get it over with.'

'Yeah, OK Steve, I got someone else to take the photo from the squat. I had to. You weren't there. At least then one of the pictures would get taken as usual. We can go and do yours now.'

'It's not the same though, is it. I mean, it's not going to be six twenty-one exactly.'

'No one will know,' said Pricey. 'You can't have changed much in an hour, can you?'

'The chain's been broken though, hasn't it?'

'Not really.'

'If six twenty-one's so unimportant, then, why did you get someone else to take your picture? Why didn't you just wait for me?'

Pricey dropped his head like a child who's pigged more than his fair share of sweets. Steve felt sorry for him, but he still wanted to punish him, even though it was his birthday.

'Well . . .'

'The whole thing's ruined now.'

Pricey was exasperated. He had tried to be reasonable, but Steve was intent on feeling sorry for himself. Pricey pushed himself away from the kerb.

'I'll see you at the bridge,' he called, 'if you're still interested!'

He wobbled away towards the junction at the foot of the hill. Steve sighed and rushed after him, catching up as he tried to turn left on to the main road to Mill Bottom.

'Wait for me, Pricey!' he laughed, grabbing hold of the saddle. 'Look, I'm sorry. I shouldn't take it out on you just because my brother's a pig.'

Pricey held grimly to the handlebars, refusing to move or look round. Power had shifted in his direction and he wanted to make the most of it.

'Pricey,' Steve continued, 'are we just going to sit here or what?'

Pricey relented.

'Let's go and do it then,' he said.

But taking the photograph was not a success. Their hearts weren't in it. A fixed smile and faked-up enthusiasm were no substitute for the real thing.

2

Steve was not properly asleep. He had not even bothered to get undressed. For a long time, in the prickly heat beneath the eaves, he had been staring at his brother's empty bed. Steve both missed and resented his brother, not just because he had gone and the bike was lost, but because he had grown up and left Steve behind. But it would be sacrilege to occupy the bed too soon. That would be confirmation that Richard had gone and wouldn't be coming back. On the other hand, its position beneath the window offered some relief from the attic's stifling heat. Then a noise outside disturbed his thoughts.

He crossed the room and poked his head out of the window to discover what it was, but he couldn't see anything. Then he heard the gate squeak as it opened. Had his brother really come home?

He waited for the scrape of the key in the lock, but instead he heard a familiar tick-tick-tick and the creak of the larch lap fence as something pressed against it.

Then there was nothing.

Steve eased himself off his brother's bed and crept down the ancient staircase, careful to avoid disturbing his parents.

He stopped at the foot of the stairs. It wasn't Richard he had heard. There was a girl at the kitchen window, her face floating not six inches from the glass. For one moment Steve thought she was going to tap on the pane to be let in, as though she had forgotten her key. Instead, she turned her attention to the window box. She rubbed a pinch of earth between her fingers and then picked up Mrs Armstrong's watering can.

Feeling that there could be little to fear from a girl of his own age, Steve crossed the kitchen and opened the back door. Startled, the girl fled from the yard, leaving Steve's bike, and scrambled up the bank into Rising Wood. With no time to wonder at the unexpected return of his bicycle, Steve set off in pursuit.

Although the girl was out of sight by the time he'd climbed the bank, Steve knew there was only one way she could go, and that was along the ridge path which marked the boundary between the wood and the Top Wold, the high plateau above the valley. Below this point, Rising Wood was a tangle of decaying trees and struggling saplings. The wood hadn't been thinned for generations and the ancient footpaths had fallen into disuse.

Rising Wood was a forbidding place even in daylight, so what the girl was doing there alone at night Steve could only guess. Although her behaviour in the yard had been odd, it had in no way seemed deranged. Steve had heard of sleepwalkers. He knew that their actions could be bizarre, but he had never heard of anyone wandering quite so far. Apart from that, she seemed an unlikely bicycle thief.

The sky above the Top Wold was barely dark, awash with both the old and the new day, but beneath the trees the path was shadowy, veined with roots. No matter how fast Steve ran the girl stayed ahead of him, just one pace out of sight.

When the distant lights of Little Dipping appeared through a gap in the trees to his right, Steve stopped to catch his breath.

The girl had halted too, concealed in the shadows, closer than before. She was toying with him. Thief! Why didn't

14

she show herself? Then she began to sing, her voice barely audible:

> Bogwitch, Bogwitch,
> filled with greed.
> Dig for her
> and we'll be freed.

Skipping song! The one that had irritated him like a prickly burr all evening. If only he could catch her! Girl or no girl, he'd choke her with leaves.

> Bogwitch, Bogwitch,
> fills a need.
> Climb the ridge
> and plant your seed.

Then the girl was off again. Steve followed but gradually lost ground. The path climbed steadily for a mile and then fell away towards the far edge of the wood where High Force, a towering waterfall, plunged into a pool one hundred feet below.

When he rounded a bend thirty yards from the falls, Steve knew he had lost her. If she had still been on the path, she would have been clearly visible against the billow of spray at the end of the tunnel of trees. Steve slowed to a tired walk and continued towards the falls.

Because of the dry summer, High Force had been reduced to one central cascade eight feet wide, which Steve could have jumped across if he had the nerve. Its winter roar had been muted, but it was still a thing of wonder. High Force had its own light. There was no night here. The dark rocks glistened in a silver haze touched with greens and blues, as if every surface had been delicately tiled with the iridescent scales of slender fish. Below the cascade, the

15

Cauldron, as the pool was known, changed shape constantly in the shifting spray.

There was no obvious path down to the pool, the rock was sheer on three sides. Yet the girl was there at the water's edge. She was pacing up and down near the Cauldron's mouth, as if thinking about crossing the rocky weir. Steve rubbed his eyes to clear them of mist. When he brought them back into focus, the girl had gone.

By the time Steve reached home, dawn had broken. His bike was still in the yard where the girl had left it. He couldn't believe that she had been the thief, but if she wasn't, where had she found it and how had she known who it belonged to?

As for her disappearance, Steve couldn't bring himself to believe that she had fallen into the Cauldron and drowned. She had probably gone on down the valley.

Steve pulled the bike away from the fence and perched on the saddle. It was undamaged. The handle-grips felt sure under his fingers. It was just as he'd last seen it, except that a frond of leaves was caught between the saddle stay and the rear wheel. It dangled down over the spokes like a pony's tail. On closer examination, he saw that the leaves had not got there by chance. They had been tied under the saddle with green gardening twine. It was just the sort of thing someone might do in a whimsical moment.

Steve took the leaves into the house and put them in water, using a milk bottle as a make-shift vase. Pleased by the effectiveness of his arrangement, he set it down on the kitchen table so that his mother could identify the leaves in the morning. Then, weary from the chase, he dragged himself upstairs to sleep on Richard's bed by the window.

*

Shortly after lunch on Sunday, Steve turned left off the High Street into the pot-holed road leading to Pricey's house, a semi-detached Edwardian villa built of yellow stone. Through the open skylight he could hear Pricey practising the saxophone in his attic room.

It was Mrs Price who opened the door when he knocked.

'Come in, Stephen,' she said kindly. 'I was hoping you'd pop round. David's been a pig all morning.'

'Yes, I can hear him,' said Steve.

'Have you two had words or something?'

'Yes, sort of,' Steve admitted. 'I was late meeting him yesterday and messed up our photograph.'

'Just like his father! He can't stand being kept hanging around either,' laughed Mrs Price.

'No, it was my fault,' said Steve, 'I got stroppy with him for not waiting, but we sorted it out, I think.'

'I'm glad,' said Mrs Price. 'I'd hate you two to fall out. You've been friends for such a long time.'

Steve fidgeted on the step, embarrassed by her confiding tone.

'Well you'd better go up,' said Mrs Price, at last, ushering him into the hall.

The Prices' rambling house always reminded Steve of a hotel – until he came to the poky staircase which led to Pricey's quarters. Here the carpet gave way to cracked linoleum. Pricey's world was chaotic and divorced from any order his parents could impose. They had given up trying a long time ago.

The floor of Pricey's room was littered with sheet music. Every other available surface was strewn with half-completed construction kits, cassettes in all the wrong boxes (if put away at all), untidy heaps of clothes and discarded toys. Wires trailed everywhere. If there was a socket in the wall,

17

Pricey made sure he set up his electrical equipment as far from the power point as possible. It was a miracle he had never been electrocuted.

'Pricey!' yelled Steve when he reached the landing. 'It's me, Steve!'

The saxophone rasped one last time and Pricey's unkempt head appeared at the head of the stairs. He jerked his thumb over his shoulder, indicating that Steve should come up. Steve took this as a sign that he had been forgiven.

'Glad you've dropped round,' said Pricey, clearing a space on his bed. 'Mum's in a bitch of a mood!'

'Oh,' said Steve, 'she seemed all right to me.'

'She always is to visitors,' Pricey laughed. 'But you should try living here! Monica couldn't sleep last night and kept going in to wake Mum up.'

Monica was Pricey's ten-year-old sister. Steve tried to avoid her because she had a crush on him.

'She's not in, is she?' Steve groaned.

'No, you're lucky. Dad's taken her and her gruesome friends swimming in Mill Bottom. Then they're going to McDonald's – I think they're trying to tire her out. They never take me to McDonald's when I suffer from insomnia!'

'Look on the bright side,' said Steve, 'they won't be back for ages.'

'Yeah, that's something,' Pricey admitted. 'What music do you want on?'

'Anything, I don't care,' said Steve, eager to nurture Pricey's benevolence. 'Look, I'm sorry,' he continued, as Pricey slotted a tape into his cassette player. 'About last night, I mean.'

'It's OK,' said Pricey magnanimously.

'It all turned out right in the end, anyway,' said Steve. 'My bike turned up!'

'What?'

'Your mum's not the only one who's been up half the night.'

'What happened?'

'A girl brought it back last night.'

'Anyone we know?' said Pricey, excitedly. His interest continued to grow as Steve told his story.

'Mum says the leaves are from a rowan tree,' Steve concluded. 'Mountain ash.'

'You reckon this girl was a mental case?' said Pricey. 'What do your mum and dad think?'

'Didn't tell them. I just said the bike was there when I went downstairs to get a glass of water. Are you doing anything this afternoon?'

'Annoying Mrs Albertson next door, that's all.' Pricey grinned. 'But I reckon three hours' practice for one day is enough.'

'Want to go out?'

'Why not. Where?'

'High Force?'

'Not been there for ages,' said Pricey, eagerly. 'I'll borrow Dad's bike again.'

'Riding that thing's like a permanent kick up the backside,' said Pricey.

They had stopped on the bridge over the Wool Water to adjust his saddle. He gazed over the parapet at the grey river bed while Steve worked with the spanner.

'Can't see any fish,' he said flatly.

'Not been any for a while,' Steve responded. 'Ramswold's going to the dogs these days.'

It was true. The Upper High Street in particular had declined in recent years. There were a number of empty shops, boarded up and covered with fading fly-posters.

'Your dad had any luck with his job advert?'

'The carpentry, you mean? No. Mum's going to try to get some extra hours though. At least that's something.'

But Pricey had already lost interest. 'Do you reckon I should get a proper bike?' he said.

'Depends on how much you're going to use it.'

'I got loads of money for my birthday.'

Pricey hadn't meant to be insensitive and he certainly wasn't bragging.

'I'd buy an electronic keyboard if I were you,' said Steve. 'Put it through the amp and give Mrs Whatsit a really hard time! Stick with the bus, Pricey, it's safer.'

'Perhaps, you're right, Steve,' he said. 'I think this bike ride's going to half kill me!'

'Don't be pathetic!' Steve scoffed. 'Let's go.'

They pedalled across the bridge to the Railway Hotel. At one time it had marked the terminus of the Mill Bottom Branch Line, which had closed long before Steve and Pricey were born. The hotel had been the pride of Ramswold, but now the gold lettering which had emblazoned a welcome across the front was just a faint shadow. The building had been sub-divided into shabby flats and then fallen into disuse. During the previous winter, squatters had moved in.

'Your brother really living there?' said Pricey.

'Don't say it!' said Steve. 'I know. He's crazy.'

They turned left into the old goods yard and rode towards the railway line which had recently been converted into a cycle path.

'God, it's hot!' Pricey complained.

'Stop moaning,' said Steve, 'it'll be cooler once we get under the trees.'

3

Pricey free-wheeled to a stop. They had almost reached the crooked finger of the Oakridge, the bracken-topped escarpment which dominated the entrance to the valley. The usual way to High Force was to climb up the escarpment on the Mill Bottom side and follow the stony track along the top.

'We going up on to the Oakridge?' said Pricey, doubtfully.

'Not unless you fancy abseiling down to the Cauldron on a rope!'

'Can't today.' Pricey grinned. 'Forgot my helmet. Now isn't that just too bad?'

But there was another way. An overgrown spur of the Mill Bottom Branch Line bore away to their left, not far from where they were standing. It would take them upstream towards Bassetts Mill. Once they were beyond the mill they would have to work their way along the bank to the pool beneath High Force.

The mill had originally been built at the foot of the Oakridge to draw its power from the stream below the Cauldron. The railway spur stopped fifty yards short of the mill, where it became a rocky track. Such poor communications didn't make sense, which was why, Steve imagined, the mill had closed down.

Pricey wasn't keen on going that way when Steve suggested it.

'I don't suppose there's an easier route?' he asked.

'You can always wait for me here,' said Steve, trying not to sound irritable. Pricey had a point. It was going to be hard-going in the heat. The line was overgrown, and riding was impossible because the sleepers were still in place on their bed of chippings.

Pricey preferred not to be left alone with the bikes on the deserted cycle path.

'I've come this far; I might as well go on. It's about time I did something to keep fit anyway.'

After they'd pushed the bikes some hundred yards, they stopped.

'We'll have to leave the bikes here,' said Steve.

Ahead of them, the railway had been overwhelmed by nettles and brambles.

'Wish we'd brought a drink,' moaned Pricey.

'There's always the stream,' said Steve.

'Got to be joking! It's probably polluted if it's come through the mill.'

'We'll have to wait till we get to the top then.'

'Dead sheep,' said Pricey scornfully. 'I wouldn't drink there either. Looks like we'll die of thirst before we get back to civilization.'

'Want to go home?' said Steve.

Pricey looked back the way they had come.

'We're nearly there. It's bound to be easier once we're past the mill. Anyway, if there's a body to be found I want to be in on it.'

'I'm sure she didn't drown,' said Steve, more to reassure himself than anyone else.

Pricey had no desire to discover a body either, but he liked to scare himself with the idea of it.

'Well, we may find a clue to who she is. She couldn't have got through this lot without snagging something. Look at the state of my arms already. I'm cut to bits!'

'Pricey, stop moaning and shove your bike into the bushes with mine. We'll padlock them together and pick them up on the way back. Take your pump to bash down the nettles.'

They pushed on for another fifteen minutes until they emerged on to the track from a dense thicket of saplings and caught their first sight of the mill.

'Blimey,' said Pricey. 'It's much bigger than it looks from up on the ridge.'

Bassetts Mill jutted out across the valley, a towering stone edifice five storeys high. One of its gable ends was embedded in the escarpment. Buddleia bushes the size of small trees had taken root high up in the stonework. Tall sycamores, uprooted from the shallow soil by winter gales, had fallen against the walls. It felt like a pitiless place.

Instead of crossing the bridge to the mill, Steve and Pricey kept to the left of the stream.

'You reckon that girl came down along the other bank?' said Pricey.

'And right past the mill in the dark? Would you?'

'Probably not,' Pricey replied, 'but if she came down this bank, where did she go after she reached here? We'd have seen some kind of trail through the bushes. And on the other side, she couldn't have made it unless she actually went into the mill and out through one of the upper storey windows on to the Oakridge. See that one on the top floor? The sill touches the slope.'

But the frame and the leaded glass were intact. No one had been through it for years.

When they reached the Cauldron, they flopped down by the pool and lay on their backs, staring up at the cloudless sky.

'*I am knackered!*' exclaimed Pricey. 'But what a brilliant place!'

23

'You do realize, Pricey,' said Steve, rolling over to talk directly into his friend's ear, 'that we are lying on the exact spot where I last saw the girl alive.'

'You're kidding!' said Pricey, sitting bolt upright.

'I'm not,' said Steve. 'Fancy a swim?'

'What? Now?'

'I'm sweating like a pig, aren't you?'

'I haven't brought my stuff.'

'Don't need any!'

'What if someone sees?' said Pricey.

'There's no one here, no one ever comes up here. Anyway what would it matter if they did?'

'Aren't we going to look for clues? And a way down from the top?'

'Later,' laughed Steve, more excited by the immediate prospect of cooling off in the pool, 'there's plenty of time.'

'Bit dangerous isn't it?'

'Water level's way down,' he said. 'Look how slowly it's going over the lip of the pool.'

'Looks like a raging torrent to me,' said Pricey.

'I'll be all right if I stay at this end. You fancy coming in?'

Pricey hesitated. He was tempted by the cool clear water, but he didn't want to take his clothes off in public.

'No, I'll just dip my feet in. It's best that one of us keeps a look out.'

Steve was too hot to laugh at him.

'Won't be long,' he said, tearing off his T-shirt and jeans.

'You're not going to take everything off are you, Steve?' said Pricey, looking up the cliff, expecting to see a host of curious spectators.

'Well, I'm not going to ride home with a damp backside, so there's no other choice is there? See you in a minute!'

With that he was gone, headlong into the Cauldron.

'Idiot!' Pricey cursed.

24

When after thirty seconds Steve still hadn't come up for air, he got up and moved closer to the edge. He had lost sight of his friend somewhere on the far side of the pool. Then the mosaic of surface reflections erupted, soaking him in icy water. Steve splashed back off the rocky platform and let himself drift towards the centre of the pool. Before Pricey could regather his composure, Steve arched his back and slipped quietly down below the surface.

'Idiot!' Pricey shouted, as Steve's feet disappeared through a ring of bubbles. He looked round for a stone to throw. But there were only large rocks to hand, and he was not prepared to risk hurling one of those in after his friend, however annoyed he felt.

The pool, beyond the immediate area of the cascade, was not much more than eight feet deep, and was shallower still where it spilled over into the stream below. Every detail of the Cauldron's rocky bed was lit with an algal green light. Trout flickered and cut the water into unimagined shapes and shadows. They were impossible to catch. Steve touched bottom. He turned to face into the current and allowed himself to be pulled backwards towards the weir. The distant explosion of the cascade pressed against his ears. He felt he could stay under for ever.

Then his toes touched metal and he was brought back to a reality he understood: his foot on a pedal. He shot up to the surface and gulped in a lungful of air. Pricey had taken his socks off and was idling his feet through the water. He waved when he saw Steve.

'How can you stand the cold?' he yelled. 'You've been down ages again!'

'I'm a natural, Pricey. It's easy if you don't think about it. See you in a minute,' he called and submerged again.

The bicycle lay on its side, the bottom bracket lodged

against a boulder. The front wheel stuck up into the air at an angle. The frame was covered in weed.

Steve broke the surface again. Pricey was drying his feet with his socks.

'I've found something!'

'The girl?' said Pricey, in alarm.

Steve laughed. 'No, a bicycle!'

'What?'

'I'll need your help to get it out . . . don't worry, I'm not going to ask you to get wet! Position yourself as close to the weir as possible. I'll duck under and drag it across.'

Steve went down again and took a grip on the handlebars. The bicycle came away easily from the bottom, but the chain had come off and the rear wheel refused to turn. Struggling to keep his head above water, he began to drag it towards the bank.

The water sucked and pulled at his legs. His feet shifted on the slippery rock. As soon as he was near the edge, he shouted: 'Quick, Pricey! Grab the handlebars before we lose it over the weir. I'll push and you pull.'

Pricey teetered forward, his arm outstretched. Steve shoved the bike towards him. Pricey's fingers tightened over the rubber grip and between them they manoeuvred the bike on to the rocky platform.

Steve began to dry himself with the end of his T-shirt. 'Wish I'd brought a towel,' he said.

'Just get your jeans on quick before anyone sees. What if that girl came back?'

'I wish she would,' said Steve. 'Then at least we'd know who she was and what she was doing with my bike last night.'

Pricey nodded, but his mind was on the bicycle they'd just retrieved from the water.

26

'Must have been in there some time. Who'd bother coming up here to chuck a bike in the water, though? If you wanted to do that you could just throw it into the Woolly along with all the other rubbish,'

'Thief?' said Steve, buttoning his jeans. 'Vandal? Accident?'

'Girls' bike,' Pricey observed. 'Bit of a posh one by the looks of it. Never heard of anyone nicking a girls' bike before, and it's not the sort of thing you'd ride through the woods is it?' He bent down and scraped at the frame with his finger. 'I mean, pink with white-walled tyres?'

Pricey was quite happy to speculate about the bike's history, but beyond that he had no interest in it.

'What we going to do with it now?' he said and then, after a pause, added hopefully, 'Chuck it back in?'

He would relish the splash. However, Steve immediately confirmed his worst fears.

'I'm going to do it up,' he said, and then seeing Pricey was about to protest, he added: 'It's all right for you, Pricey, you've got your sax. I'm going to need something to do in the holidays, particularly when you go away in August.'

'It'll take you longer than three weeks, I bet.'

'Well, I can try, can't I?'

Pricey relented. 'You'll have to carry it, though. Look at the state of it . . . it weighs a ton!'

'Tell you what, if you help me carry it back to where we left the bikes, I'll carry it over my shoulder the rest of the way. You can ride my bike, and I'll push your dad's. How does that sound?'

'OK,' said Pricey, 'just this once, but I still think you're mad. You'll never be able to do anything with it.'

Pricey was cheerful enough as he bumped the mountain bike down the spur towards the cycle path, but with two bicycles to cope with, Steve became increasingly ill-tem-

27

pered. By the time they reached even ground, Steve wasn't saying much at all.

'I told you to chuck it back in the water,' said Pricey, and then took off down the cycle trail.

'Up yours, Pricey!' shouted Steve, throwing both bicycles to the ground.

Before long Pricey reappeared, racing back at top speed. Bored by being on his own, he had returned to lend a hand.

'It'll be quicker if we both carry it,' he conceded.

'You don't say!' said Steve, but nevertheless he was glad of the assistance.

They swapped bikes and set off again, balancing their find between them. Steve bore most of the weight by keeping a grip on the saddle, while Pricey's job was to steer. They wobbled along awkwardly, but it was quicker than walking.

A mile further on, when they had reached a point just beyond Paupers' Pond, they stopped for a rest. Here the valley was at its narrowest. Paupers' Pond was a desolate place, associated with the suicides of destitute mill workers a century before. The pond itself was now no more than a breeding ground for flies and mosquitoes.

'Let's swap over,' said Pricey, 'I'll take a turn at the back. My arm's tired.'

Pricey had seen trouble twenty yards ahead, but he hadn't wanted to say so. Some distance off, coming their way, were three Dobermann pinschers, their noses skimming the ground.

'It's all right,' said Steve, 'they're on the lead.'

The dogs belonged to a tall woman with a beehive hairdo, firmly bound by a scarlet headscarf. As one three-headed animal, the Dobermanns became aware of Steve and Pricey and froze.

The attitude of the Dobermanns made Steve wary. His

28

T-shirt prickled against his back. Pricey shuffled his bike in closer behind.

As the dogs began to strain at the leash the woman dug in her heels. Unable to dash forward, the Dobermanns began to bark. Their baying echoed round the valley and, excited by the woods' phantom voices, their fury redoubled. Steve doubted that the tall woman, perched on high heels and thin as a lipstick, could restrain them.

When she beckoned Steve and Pricey forward, they pedalled towards her. For a moment the dogs calmed down. But as they drew level they began to snap and snarl.

'It's all right, they're only playing,' said the woman. Her voice was thin.

Before Steve could think of a contemptuous reply, the dog at the centre of the pack lunged forward. Pricey yelled and lost his balance, pulling the full weight of Steve and two bicycles down on top of him.

By the time they'd untangled themselves, the woman had restrained her dogs. Steve couldn't determine her age. Her face was hidden beneath a crust of foundation. She was the colour of cheap ice cream.

'You OK, Pricey?' he asked, as he righted his bicycle.

Pricey swore. Steve helped him up.

The woman with the beehive eyed them imperiously. She barely moved her thin lips when she spoke.

'You ought to be more considerate. Upsetting my dogs like that. I assume it won't happen again!'

It was clear she did not expect them to use the cycle path in future. Then without another word, she led her dogs away.

Steve was outraged, Pricey was beside himself.

'Stuck-up bitch!' he shouted.

The woman turned and gave Pricey a withering look, which Steve found unnerving, but she didn't say anything more. Then she veered off the cycle trail down a narrow path towards Paupers' Pond.

'Bitch!' shouted Pricey.

'Leave it,' said Steve, 'it's no good trying to argue with an old cow like her. Let's go.'

When they reached Ramswold, Steve waited outside Mrs Titmarsh's, the newsagents, while Pricey took his dad's bike home. The shop was in darkness, closed for the afternoon. He studied a sad collection of faded boxes which had been left in the window from last Christmas. Steve was glad when Pricey returned.

Rise Cottage was not much more welcoming when they got to the top of the hill. Pricey fidgeted uncomfortably at the gate; the Armstrongs were rowing again. Steve opened the gate loudly and let Pricey push the mountain bike into the yard.

'Stick it over there,' he said, pointing to the space where his brother's motorcycle had been before lunch. 'Looks like Richard's been back for his bike.'

The back door opened and Mrs Armstrong came out into the yard.

'Hello, David,' she said warmly.

'Look what we've found!' said Pricey, to disguise his embarrassment. Mrs Armstrong always fussed over him, just like his own mother did over Steve.

'What on earth?' said Mrs Armstrong, 'And Steve, just look at the state of your clothes!'

'It'll wash off,' said Steve.

'And since when have you been the expert?' said Mrs Armstrong. 'I expect Mrs Price never has this trouble with David.'

Pricey squirmed. If he hadn't been dying for a drink, he'd have made his excuses and fled.

4

Pricey declined an invitation to stay to tea, and when he had gone, Steve went upstairs to his room. He found a note propped up against the radio on his bedside table.

Dear Steve,
A mate of mine said he'd seen you on the bridge with your bike, so I thought I'd come and make my peace. Don't know why I bothered. Mum went up the wall again. Drop down and see me some time. Dad fixed my bike! Glad yours turned up.

Richard

Steve read the note again, then slipped it under his pillow.

Tea was insufferable – his parents started rowing about money – and he was glad that Pricey hadn't stayed. Halfway through, even before he'd started on the cake, he shoved his plate to one side and clattered up to his room.

Shortly afterwards, the back door slammed, then the gate. A chair scraped loudly across the kitchen floor, a fist came down on the table, rattling the china. There was silence for a moment and then Mr Armstrong began to climb the stairs.

'Can I come in?' he called from the landing.

'Where's Mum?' Steve asked, when his father had made himself comfortable on Richard's bed.

'Gone out,' said Mr Armstrong, with uncharacteristic

gloom. 'We're going to miss Richard's contribution. Your mum's going to have to work full time.'

'So?'

'I never wanted that.'

Stupid pride, thought Steve, but his father was of an older generation.

'No chance of a job then?' he said.

'Not yet,' said Mr Armstrong. Then he paused. 'Look, you'll have to know sooner or later. It looks like the piano factory isn't going to re-open after all. They've sold the property off to a mail-order company. We may have to move. That's what we were rowing about. Your mum wants to leave Ramswold. I want to stick it out.'

The angry exchanges between his parents continued for the rest of the week, and for once being at school was a relief. Steve kept his eyes open for the girl who'd returned his bike. He asked around but no one else had seen her. He thought she might be a gypsy, but there hadn't been any in the valley for months.

In the first week of July the rows at home became less frequent. His parents settled into an atmosphere of silent hostility, taking it in turns to be out, or watching television. Steve was able to kid himself that they were getting on better. He scanned the Situations Vacant page of the *Mill Bottom and Fallowfield Echo*, but there was nothing for his father. It was a disappointment in more ways than one. Only when things truly calmed down at home would he be able to begin restoring the bike. In her present mood, his mother would never put up with the mess he was bound to make.

When Steve arrived home after school on the last day of the summer term, he found his father leaning over the fence in the yard. He was smoking, his foot wedged in the hole Richard had made in a fit of anger earlier that year. By degrees he was enlarging the hole. The fence needed creosoting.

'What's up?' asked Steve, trying to sound cheerful. 'I thought you were trying to give those up?'

'I am. This is the last of the duty frees. There's none left after this . . . more's the pity!' he said bitterly, and spat on the ground. 'What's up? Just about every bloody thing!'

Steve hoped his dad wouldn't cry. He wasn't sure what he would do if he did.

'Is Mum home?'

'If you can call it that,' said Mr Armstrong.

'What's happened now?' asked Steve.

'Go in and see for yourself,' said Mr Armstrong. 'Perhaps you can get through to her. I can't!'

Steve didn't know how to respond now that his father was turning to him for advice. He would have liked to shoulder the responsibility and become the peacemaker, but he wasn't sure that he could. He entered the house with foreboding.

He found his mother in her bedroom. She was packing.

'What are you doing?' he asked, rather too sharply.

'You've got eyes haven't you?' snapped Mrs Armstrong. 'What do you think I'm doing? Going on holiday?'

The suitcase was jammed with a disordered array of clothing and toiletries. She had been packing in haste in the hope that she would be gone by the time he came home. Now the lid wouldn't close.

'Help me with this, will you!'

'Do it yourself!'

He slammed the bedroom door and clattered downstairs to the kitchen, but when he saw that his father was still gazing over the fence, he reconsidered and returned to his mother.

'I'm sorry,' he said wearily, sitting down on the end of the bed.

'I'm sorry, too,' said Mrs Armstrong, coming over to join him. 'None of this is your fault.'

'Isn't it?' said Steve, screwing up the corner of the duvet into a tight knot. 'It's because of the piano factory, isn't it?' said Steve. 'Dad could get a job elsewhere. I could try to persuade him to move.'

'No, Steve,' she sighed. 'I'm afraid it's not that easy.'

'What then?' said Steve coldly.

Mrs Armstrong didn't answer. Instead, she patted Steve on the knee and made another attempt to close the suitcase. Seeing that she really was intent on going, Steve helped her.

'Will you come back?' he asked.

'I don't know,' replied Mrs Armstrong.

'Who is he, then? Someone at work?'

Mrs Armstrong nodded. Steve felt he should have been more surprised by the admission.

'What about Dad?' he said. 'What's he going to do?'

'I've got to go,' said his mother, avoiding the question. 'It's not easy for me either, you know.'

'It's us you should feel sorry for – not yourself!' shouted Steve. 'Me and Richard and Dad. I hate Ramswold!'

With that, he fled the room.

His father was in the kitchen when he came down. He was filling the kettle noisily, making the pipes rattle so that he couldn't hear the footsteps above.

'Want a cup of tea?' he asked.

'No thanks,' said Steve, 'I think I'll go down and see Pricey.' He felt like a rat, running out on his father, but he didn't want to be there when his mother left.

'You won't say anything to Pricey, will you?' said Mr Armstrong.

'No, I won't,' Steve assured him. He didn't want it all round Ramswold any more than his dad did.

'I couldn't stand Mrs Price's sympathy, that's all. Sure you don't want a cup of tea?'

'No, it's OK. I'd rather go out.'

'What about food?'

'I'll cadge something off Pricey, don't worry. See you later.'

Instead of going down the hill into Ramswold, Steve walked round the cottage and clambered up the bank into Rising Wood. As he set off along the top path it began to drizzle. After going a short distance, he sought the shelter of a tall beech tree, which rose from a dry bank some distance below him. He sat down among its shiny roots with his back against the smooth grey trunk. In the solitude of the wood, which by turns hissed, whispered, shook and rattled in the dusk, he felt small and insignificant.

Somewhere, a way off to his left, the call of pheasant cut through the rain like a sharp cough. Then the wind, which had begun to whip up the slope into Steve's face, stilled for a moment and the wood lapsed into profound silence. The tree at his back had fallen to earth as a seed long before the industrial revolution came to Ramswold. What were his problems in the timeless scheme of things? Nothing at all.

He began to gain some kind of perspective on recent events. If only he had read the signs correctly he could have foreseen his mother's departure; it wouldn't have come as such a shock. Richard's going had been inevitable. It was useless to pretend that things could be what they were. The future was all. There was a father to be supported, a bike to be restored, a family to rebuild. Perhaps his mother would come back in the end, just as his bike had done. They could all try to be very grown up about it.

Then in the consummate stillness of the wood, he

became aware that something had stirred. The earth beyond the tree under which he sat was hard and compacted, almost free of leaf mould and the dry husks of beech mast. The bank, from which the tree grew, dipped sharply down on to a small terrace, which in turn fell steeply away towards the valley bottom.

On to this terrace lumbered a badger. It stopped and lifted its nose to sniff the rain which was bringing an early dusk to the wood. The old boar was a grizzled creature, and a little lame, but still capable of carrying its ribbons of moonlight and shadow into the deepest corners of the wood.

Badgers were a rarity in the Ramswold valley. Many had been slaughtered, dug out and baited by local savages and their dogs. Steve watched in awe as the badger turned its head towards him. He looked straight down into where he thought its eye must be, at the heart of its mask of dark fur. In the same instant there was a sound behind him like the snapping of a green twig. The girl in the yard! thought Steve, but the badger's head jerked sideways in pain. An air rifle! The wounded creature yelped and then bolted off the terrace into the darkness of the lower slope.

Crackling laughter spread through the wood like fire, and then died. The rain hissed down. Steve stood up and inched his way around the tree. He could see nothing. Behind him, the woods began to wrap themselves in a mantle of darkness. Angry and frustrated by what he had seen, he crept back up to the top path and made a dash for home.

5

Although he was barely able to force himself out of bed on a school day, Steve woke early on the first Monday of the holidays and went straight downstairs to make a cup of tea for his father. If they had to live alone in the house, they could at least be civilized about it.

However, his father was already up. That is to say, unable to face the prospect of an empty bed he had slumped over the table into an uneasy sleep late the night before. As Steve filled the kettle, Mr Armstrong began to stir.

'Morning,' said Steve cheerfully. The kitchen was cold and musty like the inside of a tent.

Mr Armstrong sniffed, and wiped his mouth with the back of his hand. He blinked blearily and stretched.

'You look wrecked,' said Steve. 'Do you want a cup of tea?'

Mr Armstrong nodded.

'You ought to go to bed,' said Steve. 'I was going to bring the tea up.'

'What's the point?' replied Mr Armstrong, rousing himself. 'No point moping. That won't bring your mum back.'

'What will?' Steve asked, trying to retain a note of optimism in his voice.

'Don't know. Time maybe. Or a job?'

'Will you be seeing Mum?'

'The address is over there,' said Mr Armstrong evasively.

'Well, I shan't visit her!' said Steve.

'You mustn't be like that, Steve. It's not her fault.'

'Whose is it, then?'

'Oh, I don't know. Just things, I suppose.' Then he added, 'It can't be easy living in a house full of men.'

'Going to help me with the bike?' asked Steve, to change the subject. 'I'm not really sure where to start.'

'So you are serious about that. I thought it was going to just clutter up the yard for ever.'

'Been waiting till the holidays,' said Steve. 'I thought I might try to find out who it belongs to and give it back when I've fixed it.'

'You'll need to go down to the police station then.'

That idea was not very appealing.

'They're not interested in missing bikes,' he said. 'Look how they responded when you reported mine!'

Mr Armstrong had not been impressed by their dismissive attitude either.

'How do you think it got into the Cauldron anyway?'

'Your guess is as good as mine. It's in a mess, but not too bad. Whoever chucked it in can't have done it more than a year ago.'

'So where do we start?'

'By dismantling the whole thing right down to the last nut and bolt. Each piece will have to be looked at to see whether it can be saved, then cleaned. It'll be a long job . . . and you'll do it outside, not in here. I don't want your mother coming back to find bicycle parts all over the kitchen table. When you know what needs doing, you could go down to see Monk. I'm sure he could fix you up with some old bits cheaply enough.'

Steve decided to delay breakfast until later. He gathered a selection of tools from his father's kit and went out into the yard. He studied the bike for a moment and began to make notes on one of his mother's shorthand jotters. When

38

he was satisfied with his plan of action, he went back inside to fetch his father's Workmate.

Once the bike was upended and secured, he unscrewed the chain guard and set to work on freeing the broken chain from the rear wheel. Beneath its coating of weed, it was bent and twisted. Steve examined the shattered ends. The links had exploded apart under some great shock. The chain had whipped back, chipping the paint on the chain stay and wrapping itself around the rear hub, shattering three sprockets as it locked tight. Steve called his father to help him free the wheel from the rear drop-outs.

'It's a pig,' said Steve, as his father pulled the seat stays apart to give him more room for manoeuvre.

'Whoever it was must have been going at a hell of a lick for this to happen,' said Mr Armstrong. 'They must have come a cropper. I reckon you're going to need a new rear wheel. See, the spokes are all shot at the bottom.'

'At least the tyre's not perished,' said Steve, when the wheel was safely out. The white walls were discoloured, but not cracked. The valves were intact, complete with dust caps. It was the same with the front wheel.

'Over to you then,' said Mr Armstrong, returning to the house. 'Give us a shout if you need me.'

The more Steve dismantled the bike the more optimistic he became. There might be muck and weed in every crevice, but the bike's submersion in the Cauldron seemed to have done little permanent damage. With every strand of weed he peeled away it seemed more likely that his father's estimate that the bike had been submerged for at least a year was an overstatement. Unless, of course, the rapid growth all over the bike had protected it.

By mid-morning Steve had dismantled everything, apart from the handlebars and the saddle, and allocated the components to improvised storage bins made up of an assortment of ice-cream containers, margarine tubs, yog-hurt pots and discarded washing-up bowls. Those parts which needed replacing had been flung into an untidy heap in the corner of the yard. His wrists ached, but he had vowed that he would complete the job before going in for breakfast. So, righting the bicycle once again, he clamped the frame between the jaws of the Workmate. When he had made a careful note of the frame number, he began to loosen the binder bolt which locked the seat post into the frame. The bolt was stiff, but with the aid of penetrating-oil and a long spanner, he worked the saddle free and set it aside. Where the seat post had once lodged in the neck of the tube, a twist of blue tissue paper now protruded. It was in fact the old wrapper of a tangerine, of the kind which were once rare enough to put in children's stockings at Christmas.

Steve extracted the small wad of tissue from the tube and unravelled it. He was startled by what he found. He had been expecting to find a package of spare screws or washers, or at least something to do with the bike. But instead he had discovered a silver pendant in the shape of an acorn attached to a delicate chain. He rolled it over between his finger and thumb. It glinted in the sunlight, as perfect as when it had first been polished. The acorn was correct in every detail. The cup was coarse grained and strong. The nut itself was as smooth as his mother's fingernails, except that a name had been engraved in simple script on what he took to be the reverse side. There were three letters: GEM. The girl who owned the bike? If so, it was imperative that he find her. But why had she concealed the pendant in such a place at all?

Steve went into the house to discuss the matter with his father. Finding he'd gone up to bed, he tidied away his things and rode down the hill to see Pricey.

Steve was greeted on the doorstep by Mrs Price, who promptly ushered him upstairs in the hope that he might succeed in getting her son out of bed.

'Wake up, you lazy sod!' he called, when he reached the top of the stairs. He crossed the bedroom and raked the faded curtains back along the rail.

Pricey groaned.

'What time is it?'

He propped himself up blearily on one elbow. His headphones were still twisted about his neck from the night before.

'Nearly half-past eleven,' said Steve.

'Christ!' Pricey moaned. 'Put a tape on will you, Steve, I had a lousy night's sleep.'

'Looks like it,' he laughed.

'No, seriously. Look, you couldn't go down and ask Mum to make me a cup of tea, could you, while I get dressed?'

'All right, Pricey,' Steve agreed. 'Anything to make you rise from your pit of slime!'

When he returned with the tea, Pricey was asleep again, headphones clamped back over his ears. Steve cleared a space to set down the breakfast tray, and went over to turn up the stereo.

'Bloody hell!' shouted Pricey, ripping off his headphones in a panic. 'What you do that for?'

'You'd dropped off again.'

'I hadn't!'

There was no point arguing about it. As Pricey eased himself back into consciousness, Steve told him the story of his morning and showed him the pendant.

'What does your mum think about it?' Pricey asked when Steve had finished.

'She's at work, remember?'

He wasn't ready to tell Pricey the truth about his mother just yet, though he knew it would come out sooner or later.

'My mum knows all about jewellery,' said Pricey. 'We can ask her when I'm up.'

Half an hour later, Steve took the tray back to the kitchen. Mrs Price was busy cleaning the inside of the fridge.

'I hate this job more than any other,' she said when she saw Steve hovering in the doorway. 'Just put the tray on the draining board, will you. David can wash up when – *if* – he comes down. It's about time he did something apart from squirt orange juice all over the fridge. Honestly, he's worse than Monica and her lipstick!'

'Is Monica around?' Steve asked, setting the tray down.

Mrs Price shook her head. 'Out, thank goodness!'

Steve couldn't have agreed more.

'I dread the holidays,' Mrs Price continued. 'I don't know why we bother with kids, I honestly don't. I expect your mum feels exactly the same.'

'Probably,' said Steve, noncommittally. He was relieved to see Pricey standing in the doorway.

'Anyone seen my toothbrush?' he said.

'Last time I saw it,' said Mrs Price, 'was this morning.'

'Bet Monica's nicked it. Where is she anyway?'

'Out,' said Steve.

'Good,' said Pricey. 'A toothbrush is a small price to pay for the disappearance of the loathsome Monica. What's for breakfast?'

'Dirty dishes and soapy water! And Steve, don't you dare help him.'

Pricey changed the subject.

'Any orange juice going begging? I'll need all the vitamin C I can get if Monica's been spitting on my toothbrush.'

'If you want orange juice,' said Mrs Price, gesturing to

42

the fridge, 'you'd best get a hot cloth and stick your head in here! From now on orange juice is strictly off the menu, at least until you can learn not to squeeze the carton when you get it out.'

Pricey muttered something which only he understood, and clapped the rubber gloves together.

'A musician shouldn't have to ruin his hands,' he protested.

'Gloves!' said Mrs Price.

'Bloody things make your hands stink,' muttered Pricey.

'By the way,' Mrs Price continued, 'I picked up your photos for you this morning and bought you another film to take on holiday next week.'

'Can we see?' said Steve.

'No looking before me,' said Pricey, splashing water on to the floor as he whirled round to make sure that Steve wasn't already ripping open the envelope. But there was no chance of that. Steve had always insisted that Pricey do it as long as he didn't tear the paper.

Mrs Price made some coffee when Pricey had finished the dishes, and they all sat down at the table to compare the pictures with those of twelve months before.

'Wouldn't it have been great,' said Pricey, 'if we'd worn the same clothes every year, then we could really see how much we'd grown!'

'Don't be stupid,' said Steve.

'Look,' said Mrs Price, 'I do believe David's catching up on you, Steve.'

It was true. Although they had both grown, Pricey had gained more inches. However, Steve had filled out more and was generally better proportioned, still managing to look less gauche and very much more adult.

'Fiver we're level next year!' said Pricey, as if it was a foregone conclusion.

'Done,' said Steve, 'but only if I've got the money.'

'How *are* your mum and dad?' said Mrs Price, picking up on the subject of financial difficulties.

Pricey kicked her under the table. Although he was often blind to his own lack of tact, he didn't like it when his mother was unsubtle.

'Fine,' said Steve. 'Mum's gone full time and Dad's still looking, though I suppose you know that the works aren't going to open again.'

'Yes, I was sorry to hear that. My husband was hoping to get the contract to design the new factory.'

Pricey cringed. 'Tell Mum about the acorn,' he said.

Steve was about to speak when Monica appeared in the back garden with two friends. They stretched out a length of washing line between them and Monica began to skip as the rope started to spin.

> Bogwitch, Bogwitch
> tricked a toad,
> turned three times,
> and touched her toes.

'Funny how they've taken up with that song again,' said Mrs Price. 'I've not heard it since we were kids. Monica's been humming it a lot lately.'

'What the hell is a Bogwitch anyway?' said Pricey, irritated by the song. 'That girl really gets on my nerves!'

'Better write her a new tune then,' said Steve.

'Bogwitch?' said Mrs Price, 'Don't you know? Well I suppose you wouldn't. My great-grandmother used to tell me stories about her. That kind of thing has gone quite out of fashion. All David wanted to hear about when he was younger was some rubbish or other off the television. My mother *and* my gran thought it was a lot of nonsense too and would tell her to hush up whenever she mentioned the

Bogwitch. Let's see now. How did *her* rhyme go? It was a lot less pleasant than the one we used to skip to in the street!'

Mrs Price began to chant:

> 'Bogwitch, Bogwitch,
> boiled a brock . . .'

'Mum!' Pricey objected. 'You're as useless as Monica!'

But Steve was hooked. Mrs Price thought for a moment, ignoring her son's embarrassment, and continued:

> 'steeped in sleep
> and spiced with sloth . . .

. . . or was it *stock*? I can't remember.'

'What?' said Pricey, feeling that he was being accused.

'That's what my great-grandmother used to sing whenever we lazed in bed too long. Even you couldn't lie around in bed all morning, David, if you thought someone had boiled a badger in the stuff of your dreams!'

Pricey shuddered.

'So what is a Bogwitch then?' said Steve.

'Just a character in her stories,' said Mrs Price. 'They all began: *Once there was a Badgerman and then there was a Bogwitch* . . . She had heard them somewhere; I don't think she made them up.'

Pricey yawned extravagantly.

'Come on, Steve,' he said, 'time we were going out, before Monica decides to start pestering you!'

'No, hang on a minute,' Steve protested. 'I'd like to know more about this Bogwitch thing.'

'The perfect gentleman,' said Mrs Price.

Steve blushed.

'Creep,' said Pricey, but seeing that his mother was not best pleased with him, sat down again.

Mrs Price continued: 'As I remember it, it all starts with

45

the Badgerman. He was the part I liked best. He was rather a glamorous character: perennially youthful and *very* handsome *and* extremely strong. You get the picture? According to the story, he was supposed to have roamed the four great woods around Ramswold in the company of four badgers, years and years ago. His task was to make sure that the trees grew tall and straight, that the footpaths were kept open and that anyone who got lost was found. Sightings of the Badgerman were very rare of course. That was another reason for my great-grandmother's insistence that we should get up early, so we could catch a glimpse of him coming home after his night's work. We never did see him! Very few people did, but apparently once you'd seen him, you could never forget his face, nor would he forget yours.

'Now, as I was saying, at night he would set four badgers to roam the four woods, running and snuffling after the small evils which sometimes crept down into the valley from Top Wolds or in from the vale. However, the Badgerman was not complete master of the valley. Both he and these creatures worked only through the good offices of another, a dark creature, never seen by man, but much talked about – *independent and irascible*, my great-grandmother called it, *lawless and undependable* – a vast, spectral animal of enormous power, hugely creative or immensely destructive depending on its mood. It cast a shadow over all my great-grandmother's stories. It was the Valley Bottom Badger, the very soul of all wild things, whose sett honeycombed the hillsides if you could but dig deep enough to find its tunnels and *it*, my great-grandmother insisted, *knew no allegiance but to itself*. It tolerated the Badgerman and his work, and while it continued to do so, it would have no truck with the Bogwitch.

'Of course, the small details of the stories changed each time they were told, but some things remained the same.

There was always a Badgerman and, more often than not, there was a Bogwitch who was the curse of the Badgerman's life. And where did the Badgerman come from? He was torn from the heart of an ancient tree split by lightning. *Lightning sired him and a tree gave birth to him*, is what my great-grandmother said, though sometimes she would tell us that he just appeared in the valley one day from between the roots of a great oak tree in the wake of the Valley Bottom Badger. And who or what was the Bogwitch? And where did she come from? Apparently nobody knew, or liked to think about it. Whatever, the Bogwitch began to sour the valley with her foulness. The Badgerman battled with her constantly to keep her at bay. And eventually, after many, many years, with the help of the Valley Bottom Badger, she was driven out, covered from head to toe in festering and disfiguring badger bites – that was another bit I particularly liked. What a gruesome child I must have been!

'Then, years after her going when all was well again in the valley, exhausted from fighting the Bogwitch and setting the valley to rights, the Badgerman disappeared from Ramswold and was never seen again.'

Mrs Armstrong finished her coffee and put her mug down on the table with a satisfying clunk, and looked out of the window at Monica. She began to sing again, but it was yet another different rhyme from her daughter's:

> 'Bogwitch, Bogwitch,
> caught a child,
> stole its soul
> and made it wild.'

'Well, that's basically it,' she concluded. 'That's the Bogwitch for you! Not a nice person at all.'

'What about the Valley Bottom Badger?' said Steve. 'What happened to it?'

'*It went to sleep, just like you have to now!* That's what great-grandma always said.' Mrs Price sighed and looked at Steve. 'Innocent days!'

'How come there are no rhymes about the Badgerman, then?' he said.

'Little kids like to be scared, I suppose,' said Pricey. He too looked out of the window at Monica. The chant had stopped. She and her friends were huddled round the whirligig, discussing something important.

'You were about to say something, weren't you Steve, before I started rabbiting on,' said Mrs Price. She got up to reboil the kettle.

'I found a pendant,' said Steve, digging into his pocket. He set the wad of tissue paper down on the table. 'We thought you might like to see it.'

'How exciting!' said Mrs Price, brightly. 'Where was it?'

'That's just the point,' said Pricey. 'You know I told you about that bike we found . . .'

'The pendant was in the tube under the saddle,' Steve continued. 'I mean, hidden right inside the frame. Look.'

Mrs Price came back to the table and eagerly unwrapped the silver acorn. 'It's wonderful!' she said. 'I've always wanted one like this.' She undid the clasp and made to put it on, but she hesitated. She had caught sight of the engraving. She sat down and held the acorn to the light, rolling it over between her finger and thumb just as Steve had done. 'I'm sorry, I need my glasses. They're on the sideboard, will you get them for me please, David?'

Pricey yawned and got up reluctantly.

'It says GEM,' said Steve.

Mrs Price closed her palm over the acorn and became more serious. Once more she was drawn back into the past. Pricey handed her her glasses. She put them on and held the pendant up to the light. Just then, Monica burst through the back door with her friends close behind. She received short shrift from her mother.

'Feet!' bellowed Mrs Price. Even Pricey was taken aback. 'Out, Monica! I'm busy. Don't come back in till I call!'

Monica pulled a long face, but resisted answering back when she caught Steve's eye. She flounced out, slamming the door.

'What a day this is turning out to be,' said Mrs Price. 'I think I've seen this pendant before.'

'When?' said Pricey, suddenly interested.

'When I was Monica's age.'

'You can't have,' Steve objected. 'It looks brand new, and the bike can't have been in the water for more than a couple of months.'

'Steve's right,' said Pricey. 'You must be mistaken.'

'Well then, whoever lost their bike must have acquired this somehow, because as far as I know this girl Gem has been dead for thirty years.'

'What?' said Pricey.

'I didn't really know her,' Mrs Price continued. 'She was some years older than me. I was at the primary school and she was at the secondary school in Mill Bottom. Your place. The girls' grammar school as it was then. All I remember is the pendant. She was wearing it. She came to help out at our sports day, the summer before it happened. The pendant slipped out of her blouse. I remember, because I asked if I could have it. Of course she wouldn't give it to me, because she had been given it by her father. Then after the holidays, I saw her name in the paper. She'd had an accident or something, I don't remember. I think she was a local girl.'

'She was killed?' asked Steve.

'Yes.'

'Blimey,' said Pricey. 'And you think this is the same pendant?'

'I can't be certain, but I *am* certain, if you see what I mean. What are you going to do with it, Steve?'

'I don't know, I haven't really thought about it. Is it valuable?'

'In pure money terms, I don't think so,' said Mrs Price, 'But perhaps it means something to whoever lost it.'

'That's what I thought,' said Steve. 'I thought I'd try to find them.'

'Police?' asked Mrs Price.

'Suppose so,' Steve conceded, 'but the bike's in bits, and I don't want to hand over the pendant. It would probably just get lost among all the other junk . . .'

'Else some policeman will give it to his girlfriend,' said Pricey, scornfully.

'Will you look after it, Mrs Price?'

'What about your own mum?'

Steve hesitated. He knew that Mrs Price suspected that all was not well at home. He was glad when she chose to say nothing about it.

'I see,' she said, 'you're afraid that she might think that a girlfriend has given it to you! That wouldn't do. Of course, I'll keep it somewhere safe.'

'Where Monica can't get her mitts on it!' Pricey cautioned.

Mrs Price wrapped the pendant in its paper and took it up to her room. When she came back down, Steve and Pricey had gone. Monica and her friends were in possession of the kitchen table. Mrs Price sighed and, for the second time, switched the kettle back on.

6

'That was close,' said Pricey, when they were safely out of the house. 'Monica nearly got you that time. What now?'

'Go to St Peter's to have a look for the girl's grave.'

'Serious?'

'Got any better ideas?'

Pricey hadn't, so they set off in the direction of the Upper High Street.

Neither of them were churchgoers, so when they reached St Peter's they hovered nervously on the pavement outside the lych gate. The churchyard was quiet, but they still wanted to make sure the way was clear.

'Whereabouts do you reckon the grave will be?' said Pricey, peering through a gap in the yew hedge. 'I wish they buried people in alphabetical order.'

'Don't be stupid, Pricey! That wouldn't help us either. We only know her first name. We'll just have to look.'

The hazy sky had begun to cloud over, sealing the afternoon's muggy heat. The grey churchyard looked like the ruins of something old rather than the beginning of something new, and it depressed them.

'Come on then, Steve,' said Pricey. 'I've got to be back by two for a music lesson. That doesn't give us much time.'

They passed through the dark gate and walked guiltily down the path. St Peter's was virtually as old as Ramswold itself. High on the walls, wind-chapped gargoyles scowled down at them from beneath hair-pieces of moss and lichen.

'Bogwitch, I shouldn't wonder,' said Steve, pointing at a particularly ugly example on the corner of the tower.

'Monica, more like!'

But Pricey's joke was in poor taste and they lapsed into an uncomfortable silence.

To the front and side of the church the graveyard was neatly kept. The grass between the headstones had been recently cut. Steve and Pricey wandered methodically up and down the rows. Some of the inscriptions bore a date which fitted the year they were looking for, but there was nothing for September. And none of the names looked anything like Gem.

To the rear of the church, the ground was uneven and overgrown. The first headstones leaned drunkenly in the shade of a cherry tree. The graveyard stretched away beyond, about the size of three tennis courts.

'Jesus,' said Pricey, 'it's going to be a sod to search!' Then realizing what he'd said, he looked up at the grey sky and mumbled the first lines of the Lord's Prayer. It worried him that he couldn't remember much of the rest.

'You start at one end,' suggested Steve, 'and I'll take the other.'

'No, let's stick together,' said Pricey, pressing closer to his friend.

Someone had mown a strip of grass through the middle of the untidy plot as a concession to the few people who still visited their relatives in this part of the graveyard. A mole had heaped up its mound not three feet from where the path began by the vestry door.

Steve and Pricey followed the path until it ended at the churchyard wall. They had found nothing. Pricey looked at his watch.

'Which way now?' he asked.

They began to walk back the way they had come. After they had gone about ten yards Steve stopped.

'Look,' he said, 'Let's try down here.'

He was pointing to a narrow strip where the grass had been recently flattened. The track cut a rough diagonal path towards the corner of the graveyard.

'Can't do any worse than we've done so far,' Pricey agreed.

They set off again, examining the headstones to their left and right. Eventually, the narrow path flattened out in front of a small headstone some way before they reached the corner. The grass was pressed down all around as if some one had knelt down or an animal had rolled about.

'Jemima Black!' shouted Pricey. 'This is it! See, 1ST MARCH 1947 – 23RD SEPTEMBER 1961. AGED 14. Blimey, that's the same age as us!'

Steve shuddered.

'We'll soon be older than her,' he said. 'Gives you the creeps, doesn't it?'

He turned away and walked back towards the main path.

'Where you going?' called Pricey.

'Be back in a minute!'

Pricey looked around uncomfortably, and then set to puzzling over the line which had been cut through the grass to the grave.

When Steve came back, Pricey said sadly, 'Bit neglected isn't it?'

'That's why I nicked this,' said Steve, indicating the glass vase he had found in the grass. There was an inch of green water in the bottom. 'Let's pick a handful of campion and stuff. It's the best we can do.'

When they had made their offering, Pricey said: 'Who made this path, do you reckon?' He was eager to shrug off the solemnity which had fallen upon them as they collected the flowers. He was glad no one had seen them.

'Animal, I reckon,' said Steve. 'Cat, fox. I don't know.'

Then the vicar appeared around the side of church and broke their train of thought. He recognized Pricey as the young organist he would dearly love to have, and began to walk towards them.

'I'm off,' Pricey hissed.

Steve followed his friend through the long grass and around the other side of the church, leaving the vicar with one hand raised above his head and an unanswered question on his lips.

Steve said goodbye to Pricey on the corner of his street, and went home to collect the frame number he had copied on to his mother's shorthand pad. But the police were unable to help him. The bike had not been reported missing in the past two years, and records did not go back further than that.

When Steve left the police station, he rode down the valley to Mill Bottom. Situated just beyond the mouth of the valley, Mill Bottom was similar in size to Ramswold, but there the comparison ended. Built entirely on the flat, its history had become obscured by a tangle of one-way systems and multi-storey car parks.

The library, an elegant modern building, was to be found on the site of the old Mill Bottom railway station. Steve locked up his bike in the porch and went in through the sliding doors to the grey-carpeted reception area. The enquiry desk was set in the middle of the room amidst an oasis of palms and tall potted plants.

When Steve drummed his fingers on the counter the young man behind the desk swivelled around in his chair and smiled. The VDU pulsed warmly behind him in the green shade of a Swiss cheese plant.

'How can I help you?' he asked.

'Well,' said Steve, 'have you got any old copies of the *Mill Bottom and Fallowfield Echo*?'

'Which year were you looking for?'

'September and October 1961,' he said.'

'Ever used microfiche?' the librarian enquired, pointing towards a viewer at the far end of the room.

'You mean,' said Steve, 'all the papers are stored on microfilm?'

'Yes . . . sort of,' said the librarian. 'Now hang on here, I'll be back in a few minutes.'

When he returned, the librarian showed Steve how to use the viewer. Once he'd worked out the reversed movements of the film, the examination of the *Mill Bottom and Fallowfield Echo* became easy and he soon found the edition for 28 September 1961. Then, as now, the paper came out on Thursdays. According to her headstone Jemima Black had died the Saturday before.

Steve opened his note pad and took the top off his pen. He adjusted the focus on the screen and began to read.

DEATH SHOCKS COMMUNITY

Puzzled police are still seeking the mystery hit-and-run killer of tragic fourteen-year-old Jemima Black who died on the Wood Spring bridge as she crossed the main Mill Bottom to Ramswold Road at around 9 p.m. last Saturday evening.

Jemima was found by a passing motorist, Mr J. Bramley of Fallowfield, who alerted the emergency services. Jemima was pronounced dead at the scene.

Mill Bottom High School girl, Jemima Black, of Rise Cottage, Ramswold, was last seen by her mother at 6.30 p.m. when she left home on her bicycle to visit a friend in

Mill Bottom. Police have been able to confirm that none of Jemima's friends had been expecting her that evening. Jemima's movements remain a mystery.

Police are anxious to trace what is thought to have been a grey Austin A40 seen in the Wood Spring area around the time of Jemima's death. They would also like to talk to anyone who might have seen Jemima last Saturday evening or knows the whereabouts of her bicycle which was not found at the scene of the tragedy.

There then followed a brief description of the bicycle. It was just like the one he had pulled from the Cauldron.

But what of his other discovery? The dead girl had lived in his own house thirty years before. All that time he had been sharing his bedroom with Richard, her spirit must have been lingering there.

Steve turned his attention to the shimmering photograph which accompanied the article. It was barely recognizable as the picture of a girl.

In the following week's paper, 5 October 1961, there was a post mortem report on page three. There was only one short paragraph. Jemima Black had suffered multiple fractures and died from head injuries. An inquest had been opened and adjourned until Tuesday 28 October. The funeral was to take place on Monday 9 October. There was a brief account of it in the following week's *Echo*.

The funeral was a small family affair at Gem's mother's request. The then vicar of Ramswold, the Revd Cleaver, had delivered a eulogy extolling Jemima Black's vivacious-ness, her academic ability and her sporting prowess. The headmistress of the High School had read a lesson. That was all.

It was apparent from the list of mourners at the bottom of the article that Jemima did not have a father. A Mr and Mrs

Black were listed, but they were her grandparents. There were five other names, only one of which Steve recognized – Mrs C. Titmarsh, the woman who owned the newsagents in Ramswold – nevertheless he wrote the others down: a Mr J. Brockworth, Susan Howard, Rachel Jones, Helen Farthing. The latter three he took to be Jemima's schoolfriends, and therefore would be very difficult to trace if they had married. The name Brockworth, although not uncommon, deserved further exploration.

The librarian was happy to supply the November editions of the *Echo*, and he soon located the inquest report. The jury had recorded an open verdict, but the killer driver was no nearer being found.

When he left the library, Steve hurried round the corner to the offices of the *Mill Bottom and Fallowfield Echo*, an imposing Victorian building in the gothic style. It was nearly five and they were about to close.

The woman at the counter was decidedly crabby when he approached her. She was a brusque-looking lady, about fifty years old. Her grey hair was cruelly scraped back over her scalp.

'Yes?' she said.

'Excuse me,' Steve began, 'I'm trying to get hold of a photograph like the ones in the display outside.'

The woman sighed, wearily.

'Which one?' she said. 'Football team is it?'

'No,' said Steve. He paused. 'The one on the front page of the *Echo* on Thursday 28 September 1961.'

'What?'

'Of a girl,' Steve continued. 'Jemima Black. She was killed.'

'Is this some kind of joke?'

Steve shook his head. 'No, I'm serious. I saw it in the

57

library on the microfiche, but it's not clear. I just wondered if you still kept a copy or had the negatives or something.'

The woman looked at her watch. 'We don't,' she said emphatically. 'Now, it's gone five, and we're closed.'

'But . . .' Steve protested.

A second woman had appeared behind the counter.

'What's the trouble, Mrs Tanner?' she said. Her tone was inquisitive, helpful even. She was obviously in a better mood than when he'd last seen her. It was the woman with the beehive.

'This boy's been wasting my time with some footling enquiry about an old photograph, some Jemima something or other,' said Mrs Tanner. 'If I don't go soon, I'll miss my bus.'

'You run along Mrs T.,' said the woman with the beehive, 'I'll sort it out.'

Mrs Tanner mumbled a thank you and left through the back of the office.

The woman with the beehive came through the hatch in the counter and locked the door.

'Now,' she said, turning to smile at Steve. 'How can I help you?'

Steve hesitated.

'I write for the *Echo*,' she said. 'I'm Gardenia. You must have seen my Horticultural Hints in the paper. Everyone reads them. I've just delivered this week's column.'

'Oh,' said Steve. He was not the least bit interested in flowers, but didn't wish to say so.

'Well,' the woman continued. 'You mustn't mind Mrs Tanner. It's her job to be awkward, but I think I might be able to help you. If you come with me, I'll introduce you to the picture editor. Jemima who was it you were after?'

'Black,' said Steve, but he was reluctant to say more.

The woman with the beehive handed him over to the

picture editor, who was sitting next to a terminal in a long upstairs room. She was a young woman who looked not much older than his brother, though she was probably in her mid-twenties. Then the woman with the beehive waved a flamboyant farewell to everyone in the office and left.

The picture editor smiled willingly from beneath a shock of strawberry blonde hair. Steve was tempted to confide in her, but he forced himself to be businesslike.

'I'm looking for a photograph,' he said. '28 September 1961.'

'No problem,' said the picture editor. 'What's this all about?'

'I was doing my local history project in the library,' said Steve. 'There was this girl in the paper. She was my age. A car accident. I couldn't help reading the article. It upset me a bit and I can't get her out of my mind. I thought if I saw the picture, it would stop me wondering about her. I couldn't make out her face on the microfiche. It upset me, like sometimes when you think very hard you can't remember what your mother's face looks like. She'd be about the same age as my mother if she'd lived.'

The picture editor looked at him sympathetically.

'Let's see what we can do then,' she said. 'We keep everything in our photo archive.'

Her fingers worked quickly over the keyboard of the computer.

'Got it!' she cried. 'Isn't this exciting? Let's go.'

She led Steve down to the basement where negatives and prints were stored in manila folders.

'Here it is,' she said plucking a wallet off the shelf, seemingly at random. And there she was, the girl who had been in the yard and led him a dance through the wood.

Steve folded his arms tightly across his chest to suppress

a shudder. Suddenly he loved Mill Bottom for its one-way systems and ugly multi-storey car parks, its modernity which was so reassuring.

'Blimey,' he said, 'she looks so alive!'

7

When Steve had collected his bicycle from the library, he rode round the side of the building and joined the cycle path. Now that the strange Gardenia woman seemed to have called a truce with him, the course of the old railway offered the prospect of peace and quiet to think.

The cycle path was deserted. The evening clung to the trees, airless and heavy. The path was fly-infested. Hundreds of small black lace-like flies flapped against his face and stuck to the weave of his shirt. It was only when he reached the railway bridge over Wood Spring that he found himself free of them. He dismounted and sat on the parapet to catch his breath.

Below him, the steep banks were overgrown with nettles. He tried to imagine Jemima Black crossing the road bridge. Where had she been going? He could see nothing but wood, water and the railway here.

The flies were fewer beyond the bridge and by the time he had passed Paupers' Pond, cycling was less of an effort.

At the Ramswold end of the branch line, the wood tumbled down the contours of the valley to the banks of the Wool Water and surrounded the cycle path. It was here, half a mile from the Railway Hotel, that Steve felt a sharp pain stab into his left thigh. The sting was acute, worse than any wasp. Unable to ride, he skidded to a halt. A flight of wood pigeons blundered from the branches overhead and fled across the valley towards Rising Wood.

'Bloody kids!' Steve cursed. 'Bloody stupid kids mucking about!'

Then there was an explosion of leaves high up on the slope above the railway embankment. A scream chased itself in circles through the wood, and then manifested itself as a flight of smoke-blackened bicycles hurtling through the trees.

Steve pressed hard on the pedals but his foot slipped, jolting him forward on to the crossbar. Before he could recover himself, bicycles were whirling around him, so fast that he felt he was at the hub of a spinning wheel.

When the bicycles stopped Steve found himself confronted by five riders. In the deepening shadows, they were indistinct and inhospitable figures, their faces masked by grimy balaclavas. They emanated aggression. Although they differed in height and stature, Steve guessed that they were all about the same age as himself.

They sat astride an ugly collection of machines. None of the components seemed to match. The frames were blackened and battered. Brake levers, cables and blocks – front and back – were all at odds with each other. It was as if the bikes had been assembled from a random assortment of worn-out bits. They were a repair man's nightmare, the distinctive cow-horned handlebars being their only common component.

The most powerful of the five gestured to the others with a backward wave of the hand, and in response the circle tightened.

Steve sensed the others waiting for their leader to speak. The fat boy to the right slightly behind Steve, couldn't wait.

'Shall we do him now, Savage?' he said, bumping his front tyre provocatively into the side of Steve's rear wheel.

'Shut up, Splodge,' said Savage coldly, leaning forward in the saddle.

Steve had never seen such an ugly looking gang before. They wore a ragged collection of clothing, as carelessly assembled as their bikes. They certainly weren't from Mill Bottom School.

When Savage parted his lips to speak his voice was cold: 'We don't want you here! This is our place, see. We control the line. We say who comes and goes.' He turned to the small thin boy who was clinging close by. 'It's our line. That's right isn't it, Saw?'

The boy called Saw grinned back through broken teeth. 'That's right,' he said. 'You're not welcome here. Don't come this way again, if you know what's good for you!'

'Why shouldn't I?' Steve asked. 'It's a free country isn't it?'

Savage laughed. The others pounded their handlebars with their fists.

'Free country. That's rich! Free country? Listen to him, Sniper, I don't think he got your little message. Tell him again.'

Steve felt something cold and hard prod him between the shoulder blades. The long air rifle jabbed into him again as he tried to turn round.

'No need to turn round, unless you want another message!' said the boy with the gun.

Splodge began to ripple with pleasure. 'I think he got the message the first time, Savage,' he said. 'Where'd you receive the message, eh?'

A match flared to Steve's left, sending a shudder down his spine. The half-illuminated eyes of the boy with the match were not ones you could look upon for long. He lit a cigarette and puffed on it once and then held it limply at his side.

'So, are you coming this way again?' said Savage.

'No,' Steve replied.

'Good,' said Savage. 'Now we understand each other. Let's seal the agreement. Smoky, give him a drag.'

'I don't smoke,' explained Steve.

'Smoke!' said the boy with the cigarette. His voice was gravelly. The skin just visible around his eyes was stretched. His eyes were blank. It seemed an effort for him to speak. 'Smoke!' he repeated.

'Smoky says smoke, so you smoke. It's not polite to refuse,' said Splodge, sarcastically. 'Smoke, or else!'

The gun was jabbed into the base of Steve's spine where it could do real damage. He sensed Sniper's crooked finger on the cold trigger.

Steve put the cigarette to his lips, but he was careful not to allow the smoke into his lungs.

'Deeper!'

The single word came from the boy called Smoky.

'Deeper!' he repeated.

Savage grinned.

'No!' Steve shouted.

His bike began to sway and he dropped the cigarette. The handlebars slewed about. Hands grasped his neck, searching for something which wasn't there. Then, as suddenly as they had come, the gang were on the move again in a flurry of dead leaves. Steve clung on to the handlebars as the mountain bike began to slip down the embankment, slowly at first, then picking up speed as it shot sideways from under him and careered downwards in a cascade of loose chippings. He was still clutching the handlebars when the bike exploded into the Wool Water.

He came to, gasping with the intense cold. He stumbled to his feet, waist-deep in the stream. Gardenia's three Dobermanns were snarling on the bank. At the top of the embankment was the pale figure of the woman with the beehive. The gang was nowhere to be seen.

Then someone on the opposite bank started shouting.

'Ger out of it! Go on, ger out of it! And you, Mrs, ger out of it before I do something I'll regret!'

The dogs turned on their heels and raced back up the embankment. The woman with the beehive watched motionless as the dogs lay down by her side. Then she put them on the leash and set off in the direction of Paupers' Pond.

Steve turned round and called to the small animated figure on the bank. It was his father's friend, Malcolm Monk.

'I think I'm stuck,' Steve called. 'The bike's all tangled up round these branches.'

The icy black water eddied around Steve's legs. It was an effort to keep his balance.

'Hang on! I'll be back in a tick!' shouted Monk, and ran up the bank to his workshop.

'Here, I've brought a rope,' he said. 'I'll chuck you the end and you tie it round the handlebars. Then grab hold of the back wheel and guide the bike out while I pull.'

The rope landed with a heavy smack six inches from Steve, spraying a fountain of water up his nose. He fished the rope blindly from the swirling water and with numb hands struggled to tie a decent knot.

'Done it!' he shouted at last; and then crossly, because his bones ached, 'Bloody thing!'

'Hold on,' the little man pleaded. 'It won't be long now. Right? Got a grip?'

Malcolm Monk took up the slack.

On the fifth pull, the bike lurched forward, dragging a dripping ash spar with it. The tip of the branch crunched through the spokes.

'Not to worry,' called Monk. 'We'll soon put it right.'

When Steve had steered the bike to the bank and climbed

out of the stream, he said: 'Thanks, Malc. That Gardenia woman's mental!'

'Don't know about that,' said Monk as they carried the bike towards the workshop, 'but she's an odd one all right. Her dogs are a curse on my business. She doesn't mean any harm, and I suppose she's got a right to walk them, but they don't half put people off using the trail. Anyway, what's all this about a gang of lads? I didn't see them. I only came out when I heard the splash.'

Monk opened the door to let Steve through.

'Never seen them before,' said Steve. 'They all had nicknames. They just threatened me and pushed me down the bank.'

Monk's workshop was about half the size of a school hall. Every conceivable space was taken up with the paraphernalia of bicycle-building.

'Leave your bike over there,' said Monk, 'and come into the office and get yourself warmed up.'

'So business really is bad,' said Steve, when Monk had lit the paraffin heater. There was not much sign of work in progress. The office desk was littered with unpaid invoices.

'Don't talk to me about it! Who do you think would be first to be taken on if I could afford to employ anyone? Right first time – your dad. Can't do it though. I'm just about ticking over. I thought the cycle path was going to be the icing on the cake – sales, bike hire – but no one wants to use it any more. I mean, are you going to after tonight's little caper?'

'Don't know,' said Steve. 'But I don't see why I should be intimidated.'

'You want me to call the police?'

Steve laughed.

'In that case, I think we'd best be getting you fixed up and off home before your dad begins to worry.'

66

When he had been kitted out in a pair of Monk's ludicrously small overalls, Steve followed him out to his van on the far side of the loading bay.

'Don't worry about your bike,' said Monk, 'I'll fix it for you.' When Steve hesitated, he added: 'I owe your dad a favour.'

When the van pulled up outside Rise Cottage, Mr Armstrong came out to meet them.

'All right, Rob?' said Monk. 'Just brought your boy home. 'Fraid he's a bit wet.'

But Steve's father had other things on his mind.

'What an afternoon!' he said. 'You wouldn't believe the bare-faced cheek of it. Do you know what happened? Just gone half-past five. In broad daylight and all. Two of them! Cheeky bloody kids. In the yard trying to nick that old bike of yours, Steve. And they would have except they didn't know which bit to pick up first. I saw them off, I can tell you!

'What they look like?' asked Steve.

But he already knew the answer.

8

'Gardenia? That woman again!' said Pricey, interrupting Steve's tale of the previous day's events. He bounced up and down on his bed to emphasize his next point. 'I've found out all about her!'

He leapt off the bed and rifled amongst the clutter of sheet music on his table.

'Look what I found yesterday evening,' he said, holding up a folded news cutting, 'when I was helping Dad clear up the utility room.'

Steve unfolded the clipping and studied the photograph of the woman with the beehive. Then he read aloud: '*Last Thursday Mrs Elizabeth Savage, better known to all our readers as our columnist, Gardenia, was elected Mayor of Ramswold . . .* Didn't even know we had one. How old's this, Pricey?'

'November last year. It was among the stack of newspapers we keep for cleaning out the fires.'

'It says here that she's keen to bring prosperity back to Ramswold.'

'That's a lie,' Pricey scoffed. 'My dad says that she owns half of Ramswold and most of it's empty property. He reckons she let the squatters take over the Railway Hotel deliberately because she wants it wrecked.'

'You mean she owns it?'

'Yes. It's a listed building you see and can't be pulled down. And that's not all. She owns Bassetts Mill. My dad's firm wanted to convert it to offices but she won't sell it. She could make a bomb. It doesn't add up, does it?'

'She got any kids?' asked Steve.

'What? Kids? Don't know. Why?'

'I was telling you about running into this Mrs Savage woman at the newspaper office, remember.'

Steve told him about the photograph of Jemima Black.

'You mean to say the girl you chased is a ghost?' shouted Pricey. 'You expect me to believe in ghosts? You must have been mistaken.'

When Pricey had calmed down, Steve told him about being attacked on the way home. Concluding his story, he said: 'So that's why I wanted to know if Mrs Savage had any kids.'

'If she had we'd have seen them at school, wouldn't we?' Pricey stretched out on the bed. After a moment, he said, 'What shall we do next?'

'Go and see Mrs Titmarsh,' suggested Steve, 'and find out about the funeral.'

The newsagents was deserted when they arrived. It was about to close for lunch. Undeterred, they pushed open the door and let it slam shut behind them with a resounding clang which brought old Mrs Titmarsh fluttering from the back of the shop. She was wearing a grubby housecoat, and balding slippers on her bare feet. Her hair was clamped down under a net.

'Good afternoon, Mrs Titmarsh,' said Steve, politely.

The old lady looked at them suspiciously and grunted indistinctly. Mrs Titmarsh's crabbiness was legendary amongst the Ramswold children. Even Mr Armstrong was still a little wary of her. Pricey began to have second thoughts and nudged his friend towards the door, but Steve was determined to go through with it.

'What do you want, then?' Mrs Titmarsh began. 'It's obvious that you haven't come to buy anything.'

Steve smiled. It was then that the old lady recognized

them. 'Stephen Armstrong and David Price, if I'm not mistaken. Just like your fathers. I chased them both out the shop in their time. You'd better come through to the back.'

The old lady locked the door behind them and they followed her through the bead curtains to the parlour.

'Sit down,' she said. 'I'm in the middle of making a pot of tea.'

Steve found the room comfortless and completely without cheer. It was a while before he realized what was missing. There were no personal touches to make the place a home: no mementos, no photographs, no gifts given at Christmas by children. He felt sorry for the old woman who had neither family nor friends. Only customers passed in and out of the shop her father had left to her when he died.

'So what are you after?' asked Mrs Titmarsh, when she had set the tray down.

'Well,' Steve began, 'it's a bit awkward really.'

'What he means,' said Pricey, 'is that we're trying to find out some information about someone. We thought you might be able to help.'

'Because I'm supposed to know all the gossip?' said Mrs Titmarsh defensively.

'No, that never occurred to us,' said Steve. 'I saw your name in the *Echo*.'

Mrs Titmarsh looked surprised.

'Not last week's,' said Pricey. 'In 1961.'

'12 October 1961, to be precise,' said Steve. 'It was in an account of Jemima Black's funeral. It's Jemima Black we're interested in, you see.'

The old woman closed her watery eyes.

Steve and Pricey looked at each other. The old woman was pale. They wondered if she was ill. When she opened her eyes again, she had regained her composure.

'Why do you want to find out about her?'

'I came across her name in the paper when I was doing my local history project,' said Steve.

'Rubbish,' said Mrs Titmarsh, 'you can't get away with fibs, young man. Your face wasn't made right for lies and deceit.'

Steve turned away from the old woman's gaze. 'She used to live in my house,' he said.

'That's better,' said Mrs Titmarsh. 'You've had a visit, haven't you?'

'Sorry?' said Pricey.

Steve nodded.

'On the longest day?'

It was Pricey's turn to nod his head.

'You saw Jemima too?' he asked.

'No, not Jemima. My twin brother, Henry.'

'I don't understand,' said Steve.

'He's been coming into the yard at midsummer for the past thirty years. He doesn't say anything and he doesn't stay more than a minute, but he leaves me drawings. Always on old pieces of wallpaper, done in charcoal, the poor love.'

'You're saying that your brother's dead, too, and he comes to see you every year?' Pricey tried not to sound incredulous.

'Do you mind if I ask when he died?' said Steve.

'23 September 1931, in a fire on the railway embankment.'

'How old was he?' Pricey asked.

'Fourteen,' said Mrs Titmarsh. 'He'd just left school. I've never seen Jemima, but I'd believe it if she'd started to walk. What did she bring you?'

'My bike was stolen earlier that day. She brought it back.'

'She didn't steal it!' said Mrs Titmarsh, emphatically. 'She was a kind girl.'

'Why did you go to the funeral?' asked Pricey.

Steve nudged him. The question seemed indelicate, but it was too late, it had been asked.

'She was the first papergirl in the valley, and it was me who persuaded my husband to take her on. It wasn't the done thing in those days. Boys' work, you see. He never approved. She was a very strong girl, a wonderful athlete. Such a shame.'

'Does her family still live round here?' said Steve.

'Family? Her grandparents are dead. Her mother moved after the funeral. And the father? She didn't have one, though the rumour was that he was someone local. One of those wild affairs that people only talk about when people's backs are turned. That kind of gossip doesn't interest me.'

'Do you mind if I ask you what sort of drawings your brother brings you?' said Steve.

'And why he does it?' Pricey chipped in.

The answer was just what he didn't want to hear.

'Proof, of course', said Mrs Titmarsh. 'He wants me to believe that he's really there. I'll show you. They're very odd.'

Mrs Titmarsh stood up stiffly from her chair and opened the middle drawer of the sideboard. She took out a disordered pile of papers and brought them back to the table. Steve cleared the cups so she could smooth them out.

'Have you told anyone about these?' Pricey asked.

Mrs Titmarsh sighed and raised her eyes towards the ceiling.

'People think I'm strange enough already. I have no desire to be laughed at in the Sunday papers!'

'We're honoured, then,' said Steve. Pricey hastily agreed.

'You're in the know, that's why I'm showing you. No other reason.'

'This one's brilliant!' Pricey exclaimed. 'Who's it of?'

There was something in the young eyes which Steve

recognized and it made him shiver. It was signed with the name Henry Gray.

'Himself,' said Mrs Titmarsh. 'He did that one before he died. See, it's in pencil. He could draw you so accurately that if you looked at the picture you'd think you were looking in the mirror.'

'Are they in order?' Steve asked, hoping that there would be some sort of pattern to the drawings.

'I'm sorry,' said Mrs Titmarsh, 'I'm afraid they've become rather muddled up over the years.'

They looked at each drawing in turn. They varied in subject and execution. Some were more hurried than others. Some were obviously unfinished.

'What's this of?' said Pricey, holding up a scrap of rose-patterned wallpaper.

'Sprig of rowan,' said Steve, before Mrs Titmarsh could answer. 'He's done quite a few of those. See, this one's got berries on.'

'I don't get it,' said Pricey. 'Assuming he's trying to tell you something, Mrs Titmarsh, why has he given you three pictures of a garden shed?'

'Looks like a stone barn to me,' said Steve.

'Or an old ice house?' It was the first time Mrs Titmarsh had expressed an opinion about the pictures. 'Where ice was kept before fridges were invented.'

'Recognize this one?' said Pricey.

'The Oakridge,' said Steve.

'And this?'

'The mill below it. And this one's of the tower of St Peter's,' said Mrs Titmarsh, as if at last she was getting the hang of the game.

'They're all of the valley,' said Steve, 'except the ones of the trees. He's done a lot of trees. Which one's this year's drawing?'

'Over there,' said Mrs Titmarsh, pointing to the side-board. 'I think it's on the top. I haven't got round to putting it away yet.'

Steve got up and fetched it. He laid it on the table. He was unable to say anything. It was a picture of one of the details on the corner of the church tower.

Pricey went pale when he recognized the gargoyle.

'I wish I hadn't made that joke about Monica,' he said.

'What is it?' asked Mrs Titmarsh.

'We think,' said Steve, 'that it's the Bogwitch.'

Mrs Titmarsh put her hand over her mouth to stifle a scream and then crossed herself.

'Oh, my God! What does it all mean?' she said.

That was what they'd hoped to learn from Mrs Titmarsh, but their naming of the Bogwitch threw her into an asthma attack and she had to go upstairs for a lie-down. It became apparent that they were not going to get any more sense from her that day.

9

'Do you think we should have waited for the doctor?' said Steve when they were back in the High Street.

'She'll be all right.'

'I hope so,' said Steve.

'Do you reckon Jemima Black's been visiting you every year?' said Pricey, as they set off in the direction of the church. For him the issue of ghosts was no longer in doubt.

'Don't think so,' said Steve. 'Mrs T.'s brother didn't start straight after he died, did he.'

'What do you think Henry Gray has been trying to tell her?'

'I don't know,' said Steve.

They stopped at the kerb and waited to cross the road.

'And why hasn't he just written it down like a normal person?' Pricey asked.

'Perhaps he's communicating in the way he knows best. Did you see the effort in some of those drawings, as though he had rheumatism or something?'

They found Henry Gray's grave without much difficulty. It was situated in the neatly trimmed area to the right of the church. They had walked straight past it on their first visit. The grey marble headstone was polished and the gold leaf of the inscription had been recently restored.

Pricey mopped the sweat off his forehead and looked down at the grave.

'Do you think he's actually in there?'

'How do you mean?'

'Well, I mean, if he's walking about somewhere . . .'

'Bones,' said Steve. 'That's all.'

'Let's get out of the sun for a moment,' said Pricey. 'I can't think in this heat.'

They walked back round the church and flopped down on the cool flagstones in the porch.

'Ever been in here?' asked Pricey.

'Not since I was christened,' said Steve. The confession made him uneasy.

'I used to nick money from the collection plate when I was in the Juniors,' Pricey confided. 'I'd put five pence in and take ten pence out!'

'Shall we take a look?' said Steve, nervously.

Pricey nodded. It seemed wrong just to walk away from the church without a gesture towards making amends.

'At least it will be cool inside.'

But the interior was gloomy, dusty and, at first, depressing.

'It's nice in here at Christmas,' whispered Pricey, 'when the tree's up and all the walls are decorated with branches and things from the wood.'

'Right now it gives me the creeps,' said Steve, eyeing the empty collection plate next to a pile of church histories. 'Perhaps we should go?'

'No, hang on, just for a minute,' said Pricey.

He made off down the aisle before Steve could stop him, and then disappeared behind the pulpit. A door creaked open and then shut with a dull clap like the closing of a heavy book. Steve looked around guiltily to see if anyone was coming. His eye caught the carving in the stone above the door, a sprig of rowan heavy with berries.

The first notes of the organ welled melancholically through St Peter's as, falteringly, Pricey began to play

Bach's Adagio in C Major. He stopped, forgetting how it went, then started again more confidently.

Steve sat down in the back pew and listened. Pricey played well and he found himself enjoying a sound he had disliked until now.

The stained-glass windows to the side of the church were grimy and masked on the outside by protective grills of wire. They depicted the stations of the cross in a series of gloomy images.

Then, feeling more confident, Steve got up and walked down the aisle towards the altar. Behind the altar was a large rose window with a central portrayal of Christ on the cross. Around the edge, in the upper portion, were images of the Top Wolds, and in the lower, the Ramswold woods. Shepherds and reapers populated the Top Wold, but the woods contained only a solitary figure, a young man not much older than himself who reminded him of his brother. Four dark creatures played about his feet.

He was startled when Pricey crept up behind him and said: 'What are you looking at?'

He had been unaware that the music had stopped. Steve pointed to the figure in the window. 'The Badgerman!' he said.

'You reckon that's him?' said Pricey. 'I thought he'd be a bit older than that. About twenty-fiveish.'

They drifted off to the left, towards the transept.

'Do you remember this?' said Steve. They had stopped by the font.

'It's beautifully carved,' said Pricey, fingering the grain of the oak as if it were a rare instrument. He let his hand run down over the smooth pedestal towards the floor. 'It's just like the trunk of a tree here,' he continued, 'without the bark. See, it's even got roots which go right into the floor.'

While Steve fingered the delicate patterns ingrained in

the wood on the outside of the bowl, Pricey groped around the back. He called to Steve to join him on the floor.

'Look,' he said.

'What is it?'

'The craftsman's signature.'

'Let's see.'

Pricey moved aside.

'It's crossed saws, in relief,' said Steve, 'and there's something else.'

'A date, I think,' said Pricey, 'but I can't read it.'

Steve peered again. '1841,' he said.

'One hundred and fifty years old!' said Pricey.

'1931, 1961,' said Steve, 'and 1841.'

'What?' asked Pricey.

'I don't know exactly. But there's an inscription too. I can just trace the letters with my fingers. I'll call out the letters one at a time.'

When Steve eventually stood up, he felt dizzy from bending his head at an awkward angle, but they had the message: *All's Well in Ramswold, All's Well in the World.*

'That's what my dad used to say when he put us to bed as kids,' said Steve. 'There's a pile of guidebooks at the back. Let's take a look.'

'What for?' asked Pricey.

'About the font, you idiot,' said Steve, towing Pricey off towards the back of the church. 'There's bound to be something.'

They took a guidebook each and thumbed their way through the twenty-four closely typed pages. The booklet was illustrated with pen and ink drawings and the occasional black and white photograph.

It was Pricey who found the reference first. 'Listen to this, Steve,' he said breathlessly.

'The font of St Peter's was commissioned from the carpenter Joseph Tanner of this parish, in 1841, and is believed to be the work of his apprentice, Nathan Sawyer (1827–41), and the cause of a rift between the boy and his master, the apprentice having carved his signature on the font before he had served his full time, thus showing up the talent of his master as inferior. Joseph Tanner demanded that the font be removed. The Reverend Charles Allen is supposed to have settled the matter by asking the forester Mr John Brockworth, who felled the tree, said to have been Ramswold's oldest oak, to decide between Nathan Sawyer's font and an alternative offered by his master.'

'Hang on, Pricey,' Steve interrupted. He took his list from his pocket. 'Look, same name as at the funeral. Do you think he's a descendant of this Brockworth in the guidebook? Same initial, even.'

'Probably,' said Pricey, 'everybody seems to be related around here. But there's more. Listen:

'This became a source of grievance between the two men and shortly afterwards Mr John Brockworth is said to have left the valley. The font remains as a permanent memorial to Nathan Sawyer whom it is claimed was drowned in mysterious circumstances in the Cauldron below High Force at the end of September in the same year. Joseph Tanner was put on trial for murder but the case was not proven, because no body was ever found. Joseph Tanner's descendants live in Ramswold to this day.

'Nothing about the motto,' said Pricey, when he'd finished reading. 'Fancy being christened in a dead boy's font! It's enough to give you the creeps.'

'This whole place is weird,' Steve agreed. 'Have you seen that carving above the door? It's the same as the one in Henry Gray's drawing. Do you think Nathan Sawyer did that too?'

Pricey looked up.

'No,' he said, flicking the pages over, 'but I'm sure I saw something about it back a bit. Hang on. Yes, here it is.' He ran his finger over the glossy page. 'The legend, it says here, is that it was done by the Ramswold Badgerman when St Peter's was first built, or done on a stone earlier than that, which was then incorporated into the design. The carving is thought to be a protection against evil spirits. I bet there's loads of copies up and down the valley.'

'Maybe,' said Steve.

'Shall we buy one of these things, then?' asked Pricey. It was an easy penance for the money he'd stolen from the collection plate in the past. 'How much do you think I should put in? It just says "Donations".'

'How much have you got on you?'

'Fiver,' said Pricey, doubtfully.

Steve looked at him. There was no change on the plate.

'Oh, all right then,' said Pricey, shrugging his shoulders.

He dropped the five pound note into the plate and led Steve swiftly out into the sunshine before he changed his mind. They wandered round to the other side of the church and sat down with their backs against Jemima Black's headstone.

'Do you think she'd mind us doing this?' said Pricey.

'Would you?'

Pricey shook his head.

'Dates,' said Steve.

'What?'

'There's some missing. Jemima Black 1961, Henry Gray

80

1931, Nathan Sawyer 1841. All in September. I bet Nathan Sawyer was drowned on the 23rd too.'

'Coincidence,' said Pricey.

'No point trying to kid yourself just because it's a hot sunny day and everything looks all right in Ramswold.'

'All's Well in Ramswold, All's Well in the World!'

'Wish it was,' said Steve. 'Think, Pricey! Which dates are missing? It's important.

Pricey had no trouble with maths. '1901 and 1871.'

'Five deaths!'

'So?'

'Don't you see? Come September there's going to be another. The next thirty years will be up.'

'One every generation!'

'Exactly.'

'But why? And since when?'

'I don't know. There must be two more graves. We've got to find them.'

'But,' said Pricey, 'there might be more than two.'

'Let's just start with the gaps,' said Steve.

'How many times are we going to have to do this?' Pricey complained, as they began to scour the graveyard. 'It's too hot.'

'Until we find them.'

'What if they're not here at all?'

'Where else would they be?'

'Little Dipping,' said Pricey and then regretted his words, because Steve was immediately enthusiastic.

'We'll go there next,' he said.

It was with a sense of inevitability that they entered St Thomas's churchyard in Little Dipping. There was only a small patch of ground to explore and up against the rear wall, where the slope fell away sharply towards the Ramswold valley, they found what they were looking for. Leaning lopsidedly where it had been abandoned next to a rusty wheelbarrow was the headstone of one Adam Hoggis (1857–71). Thomas Smith (1887–1901) was not far away.

'Same day, same month,' said Pricey.

'Autumn Equinox,' said Steve, pensively, 'when the length of night equals the length of day and the balance is tipped towards winter.'

Pricey sat down on the churchyard wall. He was eager to dispel their gloom.

'Brilliant view from here.'

The four great woods lay all about them, while the broad shoulder of the Oakridge reared up to the east, bathed in sunlight.

'You fancy going up the tower while we're here?' asked Steve. 'There'll be an even better view from up there.'

When they climbed through the narrow door at the top of the tower, it was like emerging on to the deck of an ancient ship. A gentle breeze sprung up to ruffle their hair.

'There's going to be a change in the weather I reckon,' Pricey observed. 'Rain from the south-west. Could well get a storm tonight. We shan't be able to do this again in a hurry.'

They sat down on the warm lead of the gently sloping roof and looked across the valley in the direction of Whispering Wood.

'What's that house down there between the Woolly and the cycle path?' asked Pricey.

'Must be near Paupers' Pond,' said Steve.

'How the hell do you get to it?'

'Must be a tunnel under the cycle path.'

'It's got a lot of land,' said Pricey. 'Who do you think owns it?'

'That Gardenia woman, I shouldn't be surprised.'

'Never knew there was a house down there.'

'Want to take a closer look?' asked Steve.

Pricey looked at his watch.

'We've got time,' said Steve.

'What about the dogs?'

'They're bound to be chained up. We needn't get too close.'

'Bit risky,' Pricey insisted. 'Better wait till Thursday evening.'

'Why?'

'Parish Council meetings are on the first Thursday of the month. 1 August, Steve, it'll be 1 August tomorrow, and I'll feel much safer knowing that she's out. I'll go with you then, I promise.'

'OK, Pricey,' Steve agreed, 'but no backing out!'

10

All that night thunder shook the valley, Steve woke twice in the early hours with the feeling that Rising Wood was astir with hunting dreams.

Wednesday dawned grey and blustery. Steve rolled over in bed and fingered the sprig of rowan that Jemima Black had left tied to the saddle of his bike. He had kept it in water beside his bed for weeks. Although it was now no more than a forlorn looking twig he hadn't the heart to throw it out.

Rise Cottage had been spared the damage much of Ramswold had suffered during the night. Elsewhere, chimneys had toppled, slates had been borne off by the wind and trees had fallen against the sides of houses.

When Steve called on Mrs Titmarsh he found her leaning on a broom in the doorway of her shop. She was fully recovered from her fit of the day before, but was unable to give Steve a satisfactory reply to his enquiry about Mr Brockworth and the other names on his list. Fearing to provoke another asthma attack by mentioning what they had discovered, he said goodbye and went round to the bicycle works.

Monk was sitting in the loading bay sipping tea from a chipped pint mug.

'Hi, Malc,' said Steve, cheerily.

Monk returned his greeting with a weary smile.

'What's up?' asked Steve. 'Roof leaked or something?'

Malcolm Monk swallowed a last mouthful of tea and

flung the rest into the nettle patch behind him. 'Something like that. Best come in, Steve, and take a look.'

Steve followed him inside.

There was a heap of broken glass and splintered wood where Monk's office had been on his last visit. Bicycle parts littered the workshop floor. Frames had been torn from their racks and hammered out of true.

'Who did this?' said Steve, casting his eye over the wreckage for his own bicycle.

'I don't know,' said Monk, 'some young bastards. And the police don't bloody care!' He kicked out at a twisted gear set, sending it skidding across the floor. It came to rest in a heap of torn cycling magazines. 'You must be wondering about that bike of yours.'

'Well, yes,' Steve replied, uncertainly.

'I took it home with me last night to finish it off. It's in the back of the van.'

Steve's relief was visible, but Monk was kind enough to pretend not to notice.

When they'd retrieved his bike, Steve said: 'Sure there's nothing I can do here to help?'

'No,' said Monk, 'I can't touch anything until the police arrive, if they ever do. Anyway, you'd better be off.'

When Steve rode up to Pricey's gate, Mr Price was coming round the side of the house holding a heavy hammer. He should have been at work.

'Hello, Mr Price,' he called, 'is David in?'

'Gone to his grandmother's for lunch,' said Mr Price curtly.

'When will he be back?'

Steve had asked politely, but Mr Price nearly bit his head off: 'How am I supposed to flaming know?'

Although Pricey's dad was always a little aloof, Steve had never known him to be rude.

'Now, if you'll excuse me, Stephen,' he said, 'I've got a lot to do, clearing up last night's mess.'

Pricey's grandmother lived in the old Ramswold Brewery which had been converted some years ago into old people's flats by Mr Price's architectural practice.

It was Monica who answered the door. She grinned shyly at Steve and then ran giggling across the hall into the lounge. When Pricey appeared, he wore the look of somebody at the end of his tether.

'Am I glad to see you,' he said, and led Steve across the cobbled yard to the other side, well out of earshot. 'Talk about being bored! Anyway, what's up?'

Steve told him about his visit to Monk.

'So you reckon,' said Pricey, 'that those kids who beat you up smashed up Malcolm Monk's, because they were after your bike?'

'Yes,' said Steve, 'or else it was some kind of revenge for helping me out. I don't know. I can't get things straight in my head. I keep thinking about the church and Mrs Titmarsh's drawings. Five dead kids.'

'Five riders, you mean?'

'Exactly.'

'Bloody hell!'

'It's Savage who puzzles me, though,' said Steve. 'I can see that Henry Gray would be Smoky, that Nathan Sawyer could be Saw. Hoggis is Splodge, that's possible. Smith – well, Sniper – has a gun.'

'Possible,' Pricey conceded. 'And your Jemima Black was trying to tell you something about them?'

'Maybe, but what about Henry Gray? If he's one of the gang why should he visit his sister every year? I mean, he seemed to be saying something about the Bogwitch story, didn't he? I have this feeling about it, like I've got a tune in my head but I can't remember the words. I can't work it out. That's why I think we should go down to Paupers' Pond this afternoon. Something's going on, Pricey, and we shouldn't delay. The sooner we understand the better prepared we'll be.'

'For what?'

'For whatever needs to be done.'

'It beats me,' said Pricey. 'What you're suggesting is that this Gardenia person is mixed up in what's happened to you, that Savage really is something to do with her? You're crazy.'

'Well, she was there when I got done over!'

'Afterwards,' said Pricey, 'after the gang had thrown you in the Woolly. Ramswold's full of nutters like her. Always complaining about something.'

'I know, but will you at least come with me this afternoon? We needn't get too close. I just want a look at the house.'

'I don't know, Steve, my mum's not too happy because Monica's been having nightmares again and my dad's in a right foul mood.'

'I know, I met him. What happened?'

'The wind blew the coal chute doors right off their hinges and let the rain into Dad's workshop in the cellar. All his power tools were ruined.'

'We've got to talk about this,' said Steve, thinking of Monk's bicycle works.

'Oh, come on, Steve!' Pricey yelled, thumping the wall with his fist. 'Now that is being ridiculous. What the hell would those kids want in my house? Was yours done over?'

Steve shook his head.

'Well then, it was nothing but the storm.'

'What time did it happen?' asked Steve.

'Just before it got light. It woke us all up. Why?'

'Monk took my bike home with him last night. He lives in

Mill Bottom. They missed the worst of the weather. Mrs Titmarsh told me.'

'So?'

'The bike was out of their reach. They could have thought I'd picked it up from Monk earlier and left it in your cellar!'

'But why would you do that?'

'For safe-keeping?' Exasperated, he ended up snapping at Pricey: 'Are you going to come with me or not?'

Pricey hesitated. He knew that if he didn't go, he risked another rift in their friendship.

'All right. But for God's sake let's stay well clear of trouble. You can leave your bike at my house, if you still think it's still safe, that is.'

When they reached the Duck and Enter Inn just beyond the junction of the main road and the lane to Little Dipping, they slipped through the side gate and picked their way across the garden to the riverside path which had, at one time, connected all the mills in the valley bottom. Towards Paupers' Pond the path was overgrown with nettles, and by the time they neared Gardenia's cottage any semblance of a right of way had disappeared altogether. To mark the boundary of Paupers' Pond, three strands of barbed wire had been strung across the stream.

Steve crouched down in the mud by the fence and indicated that Pricey should do the same. Between them and the cottage was an open tract of spiky bog grass, at the centre of which was an ancient pollarded willow. To the left of the cottage was a windowless stone shed, damp with moss and algae. In more recent times, double doors had been set into its front wall. They were stoutly padlocked at the top and bottom.

'The ice house!' said Steve.

'Let's go back,' whispered Pricey.

'We can't,' said Steve, 'not now. Henry Gray meant someone to have a look. We can't let him down, Pricey.'

'What about the dogs?'

'Can you hear them? She's probably taken them for a walk.'

Before Pricey could raise any further objections, Steve ducked through the fence and raced across the garden to the rear of the outhouse. When he was sure that the coast was clear, he left the shadow of the shed and skirted the cottage. It had been recently renovated. Each room was masked by pale venetian blinds.

He tried the front door, but it was locked. He crouched down and looked through the letter box. The hall was like a hundred others, gaudily carpeted and smelling faintly of furniture polish and lavatory cleaner. He snapped the letter box shut and stood up.

Footsteps crunched on the drive behind him.

Steve whirled round. It was Pricey.

'Place is deserted,' said Steve.

'Any joy with the shed?'

Steve shook his head. 'Let's take another look.'

'All right, but make it quick,' said Pricey, 'she's bound to come back!'

When they reached the shed, Steve focused his attention on the double doors. 'She doesn't use it as a garage any more,' he said. 'No tyre marks.'

'It hasn't been opened for ages,' said Pricey. 'The padlocks are all rusted up. What do you reckon's in here?'

'Only one way to find out,' said Steve. 'I reckon a little bit of storm damage is in order!'

'What do you mean?'

'By the time we've finished, Gardenia's going to be a few tiles short of a roof, just like the rest of Ramswold. If we rip them off the back, she won't notice.'

Pricey looked round uncertainly.

'It won't take long,' said Steve, 'if you give us a bunk up.'

The red pantiles were slippery with moss.

'Don't go too far up!' Pricey called, as Steve steadied himself on the roof. 'Breaking your neck is all we need!'

'Don't worry,' said Steve, 'I think I can get some of the lower ones loose.'

He wedged his finger-nails under a tile where it had been chipped by successive frosts.

'Come on! Come on!' he urged it.

The tile scraped sideways, allowing him to take a firmer grip. He pulled it sharply up and backwards. Pricey stepped back and shielded his face. The tile scudded off the roof and shattered at his feet.

'Careful, Steve!' he called.

The second and third tile came away more easily. Pricey gathered up the pieces and flung them wildly downwind.

Steve took careful aim at the gap he had created and punched a hole through the roofing felt.

'What can you see?' called Pricey.

'Nothing yet,' said Steve, 'I've just got to tear the felt back a bit. It's too dark . . .'

The smell convulsed his throat. He clapped his hand over his mouth and turned away to stop himself being sick. A bluebottle caught in his hair and buzzed angrily at the entrance to his ear. He slapped his head hard and the noise stopped.

'What is it?' yelled Pricey. Then he too caught the stench and reached in his pocket for his handkerchief. Meanwhile Steve had stripped off his T-shirt and wrapped it over his nose and mouth like a bandana. He began to rip away more tiles, not caring where they fell.

'What is it?' Pricey called again.

'Bones! And pelts. Hundreds of skins!'

90

They filled half the shed to a depth of about five feet. Here and there skulls protruded from the folds of decaying skin and mouldering fur.

'Badgers, I think.'

There was something else, bulky and unmoving, at the other end of the shed.

But Pricey had stopped listening to Steve's bewildered commentary.

'Steve, someone's coming!' he hissed.

Steve rolled over and slid down the roof, scattering tiles before him.

'Austin A40, Pricey!' he said, unable to concentrate on anything else. 'Grey. The one which killed Jemima Black. Pricey, Gardenia's evil! I knew it!'

Pricey looked at Steve in horror, but he was equally terrified by something else.

'The five riders,' he said. 'Listen. They're coming down the drive!'

Steve pushed Pricey round the corner of the shed and together they raced back across the garden to the bank of the Wool Water. When they reached the fence, Steve shoved Pricey through.

'Go, Pricey,' he said. 'They want me. I'll lead them off. Run to the pub. Don't stop. Get the bus home from there. Go!'

Pricey was too terrified to argue and vanished into the nettles just as the riders skidded round the corner of the cottage. And Gardenia was not far behind with her dogs, her hair a whirlwind of bitter candyfloss.

The Bogwitch was back. That's what Henry Gray had been struggling to say to his sister for the past thirty years. That was what he and Pricey had to believe.

For a moment, Steve was transfixed against the fence. Then, as the bikes cut five lines across the face of the bog grass, he moved quickly out across the stream, his feet on the bottom strand of barbed wire, his hands gripping the upper. The fence swung and bounced, but he held on. By the time he was half-way across the stream the bicycles had come to a halt on the bank. Realizing that the riders were in a quandary, Steve stretched a hand out towards the trailing branches of a willow on the opposite bank. He grabbed the willow fronds and swung shorewards as the Bogwitch barked her orders. He dropped into the water a foot short of the muddy bank and sank up to his shins in gravel. The Bogwitch let out a high-pitched screech which set the willow rustling. But Steve was already clambering out, and before the Bogwitch could get the gang organized he was running towards the cover of Whistlers' Wood, heading for a dense thicket of ash poles.

11

Steve considered his options. If he made for the Duck and Enter he would draw attention to Pricey. On the other hand, flight along the exposed top path was too risky. Making directly for the church at Little Dipping was the only possibility.

He pushed his way out of the thicket and cut a zig-zag course through the saplings and fallen branches which choked that part of the wood. Fifty yards on, he stopped and crouched down in the shade of a hawthorn bush. The fat boy Splodge was sitting astride a fallen ash trunk, his stubby legs dangling down its mossy flanks. He was supposed to be keeping watch, but was more interested in poking a stick under the bark to torment the ants.

Steve slipped away into the trees to his right, intending to forge a diagonal path across the face of the slope, but he soon discovered that the way was barred by Saw, standing in the shade of a diseased sycamore.

Steve was forced to scrabble up the steep slope towards the path along the top of the wood. The more breathless he became, the more noise he made and so his panic grew. He cried aloud as brambles tore through his sodden jeans and hooked into his shins. Then, as the shouts of the fat boy and Saw filled the woods, he tore himself free and scrambled on up the hill until eventually, gasping for breath, his fingernails torn and bleeding, he stumbled out on to the top path and staggered off in the direction of Little Dipping.

Laughter rippled behind him and then faded, only to be

replaced by the sounds of wheels whirling through leaf mould and beech mast. At first they were far behind him, then they crept further ahead and died away. Steve stopped and bent double, to rest, hands on thighs.

A twig snapped somewhere in the wood. An air-gun pellet grazed his right ear. He turned to run back the way he had come but the fat boy was advancing up the path on his bicycle. Branches crackled to his left, and down from the Top Wold came the burnt boy and his companion with the jagged grin. Steve broke into a run. The gang laughed and called to him through the wood.

'Come on, Steve! Wait for us! Oh, don't go, Steve, wait for us!'

The voices rang with a mocking sadness. There was a desolation in their sarcasm. Had he been in the safety of his attic room he could have felt sorry for them.

His step faltered, but he stumbled on, afraid to look over his shoulder. Another pellet slammed off his thigh. The calls came again.

'Steve! Please! Wait for us!'

The wind whipped up suddenly from the valley bottom and raked through the wood, intent on turning everything inside out. His four pursuers began to steal the ground from under him. They accelerated fast and drove him nearer to Savage who had suddenly appeared from the wood to block his path.

It was pointless to go any further. The bikes circled him once, then stopped. Savage pedalled closer.

'Do him, Splodge!'

The fat boy grinned beneath his ragged balaclava and cast his bike aside. 'My pleasure, Savage,' he said, grabbing hold of Steve's collar and forcing him to the ground. 'Shall I sit on him?'

'Whatever you like,' laughed Savage.

The woods crackled about Steve's ears as the fat boy settled his full weight upon him. His breath blew cold into Steve's face. It smelled of mushrooms and damp earth.

Splodge ground Steve's head sideways into the mud and tore at his throat. Out of the corner of his eye he saw the boy with the air rifle twitch and point the gun at his face. He twisted his head away sharply; the pellet hissed into the earth beside him. Steve struggled, but couldn't force the fat boy off. He sensed that it wouldn't be long before the others joined in the fray to search for what they were after.

'I haven't got it!' he screamed. 'Nor has Monk, nor has Pricey! And I'll bloody kill you, Adam Hoggis, before I tell you where it is!'

The fat boy hesitated for a moment and relaxed his grip. From beneath his balaclava came the faintest of grins as if he'd just been told a very funny joke, but couldn't quite understand what it meant.

Steve shrugged him off and grabbed the front wheel of the nearest bike, tumbling Savage out of the saddle. The others backed off a couple of feet. Savage rolled over and spat, the mucus turning to ice before it hit the ground.

Steve lunged across the path. His hands closed about Savage's throat. The pained red eyes beneath the balaclava made him uneasy. Savage's body was cold, but beneath the jumble of old clothes it was soft. There was no need to rip the balaclava upwards. He mouthed her name, hardly surprised. He didn't hit girls. Maybe he would have to learn if he was to defeat the Bogwitch. What had she done to make Jemima Black like this? She barely responded to her name when he spoke to her again.

'Gem!'

The gang were perturbed. They stood open-mouthed under the trees. Steve loosened his hold on the girl and took off in the direction of Little Dipping. Savage recovered from her daze and shouted an order.

But it was not the gang he had to fear for the moment. They kept their distance. The dogs were on the loose.

He saw the first of the Dobermanns waiting on the path, where he himself had stopped to catch his breath the night he chased Gem through the wood. In the second before the dog saw him, he made a dash down the slope towards Little Dipping.

Fifty yards below him was the source of the Dripping Stream, which the local children called Old Lardy. The spring marked the boundary between the two northern woods, and flowed downhill to the far end of the church-yard wall at St Thomas's. Eventually, Old Lardy joined the Wool Water on the Ramswold side of the Duck and Enter.

The Dobermann snarled and tore off in pursuit. Steve reached the stream with the dog five paces behind. Old Lardy, after the heat of the summer, was not much more than a trickle. Steve leapt into the ditch and continued downhill, careful to keep his feet in the water when the stream bed broadened.

The Dobermann sniffed at the nub of the spring and howled. Its call was met by the others and they closed in on the stream. But the three dogs were reluctant to get their feet wet. Instead they stalked along the bank, two on the Ramswold side and one on the other, never more than a leap away from where Steve walked, his breathing barely controlled, his panic hardly restrained. His nerves were stretched, and he fought the impulse to flee back upstream into the wood.

When the wood ended, it did so abruptly at the edge of a small meadow enclosed by a crumbling dry stone wall. The stream ran through a low arch, no more than nine inches high, set into the foot of the wall. The dogs waited on either side, poised to spring if Steve should try to ease himself over. He wanted to scream for help, but there was no one there. He had no alternative but to dismantle the wall.

So, taking the sharpest stone from the top of the wall he flung it at the dog to his left. It leapt aside, then returned to its place. Although he managed to hit the dogs several times as he took the wall apart, they refused to move. They just waited, powdered with yellow dust.

For two minutes Steve stood stock still, staring the dogs down. Then, in a frenzy, he thrashed the stream with his hands and feet, showering the wall in cold spring water. The Dobermanns snarled and lashed their heads about, but they backed off a yard. Half a second was enough, and he was through the gap, sprawling face down in the stream.

Now was not the time to make a run for the church on the other side of the field. He couldn't risk another fall, he didn't dare step out of the narrow stream. The grassy banks were exposed; the Dobermanns could come very close.

He stood up in the water and waved his arms angrily at the dogs just as Monk had done. 'Gerroff! Gerroff out of it!' But when he set off again, they continued to track him along the bank, their gaze hungry and cold, muscles fine-tuned to kill. The Bogwitch, he thought, might have chosen dogs with more guile. Nevertheless, they were persistent and waited for him to fall. Steve, like a child refusing to look down as it walked along the top of a high wall, kept his eyes straight ahead and tried to fix his gaze on the church clock. But he was unable to bear looking at it for long, and stared instead at the weather vane at the top of the tower. A representation of Old Father Time it was not. It wasn't a scythe which the figure carried over his shoulder, but an axe. He and Pricey had been too busy to notice. The image of the Badgerman gave him heart. While he remained alert to any changes in the behaviour of the stalking dogs, he found himself protected within his thoughts.

If there was a Bogwitch, then there had to be a Badgerman. But where was he? The stories said he had gone away. Surely if he had returned he would have done something about the Bogwitch. And where was she? He didn't understand her or what she was trying to do. She wanted the acorn pendant, but what for? Its resting place must have remained hidden until the day he and Pricey pulled the bicycle from the water. Gem must have hurled it in the night she died, having first put the pendant in the frame of the bike for safe-keeping. And if she had done that, perhaps the Bogwitch had been after it even then?

The churchyard was still some distance away. The dogs showed no sign of relenting. Steve concentrated on his thoughts.

But why *would* the Bogwitch want something given to Gem by her absent father? And why hadn't she been able to retrieve the pendant from the Cauldron? The bike had been thrown into the Cauldron thirty years before and had been miraculously preserved. There lay part of the answer. Perhaps the Bogwitch could not go there. And in Gem's heart was there also some place that the Bogwitch could not invade, where a secret could be kept safe? Did Henry Gray and his companions also retain some virtue that the Bogwitch could not twist to her own purposes, which allowed them briefly to become themselves once again on Midsummer's Eve? Had Gem visited him at midsummer just to show him where to find the bicycle or had she been trying to tell him more? One thing was clear: the Bogwitch was back and the Badgerman had to be found, quickly.

Then the churchyard wall was close. The stream flowed past it like a moat. The dog on the left-hand side couldn't hope to follow once Steve had passed the corner of the wall, but the other two stooped and inched forward on splayed claws.

'Gerroff with you!' Steve shouted again.

With the dogs almost at his heels he hauled himself up on to the wall, tumbled down the other side and hurtled towards the tower.

Only when he had reached the top did he feel safe. The dogs had separated again and taken up positions around the churchyard, ready to shuffle out of view if anyone appeared on the road.

Steve lay down wearily against the roof and allowed the late-afternoon sun to dry his clothes. He would wait until the vicar arrived to lock up.

12

When Steve woke, he found himself in shadow. He looked at his watch. It had stopped. Beads of moisture clouded the glass.

The vestry door slammed, a key rattled in the lock. Steve moved stiffly to the edge of the tower, but he found he was on the wrong side to draw the vicar's attention. By the time he'd worked his way round the roof the vicar had gone. Little Dipping was quiet except for the hiss of a sprinkler in the rectory garden. He couldn't see the dogs, but he knew they were there.

Steve looked up at the weather vane – the Badgerman with his axe. The arrow was pointing to the south-west, to St Peter's. There had to be a way out. If he sat around waiting for rescue, the Bogwitch would find Pricey and the pendant and it would be too late.

Steve descended to the nave of the church. The interior was simpler than St Peter's. The stone floor was well worn and the pews highly polished. The stained glass was clean but nondescript. It was a quiet, unshocking place, which confirmed belief and offered no challenges. God was familiar here, he did not sit in judgement.

There was another door at the foot of the tower. Above it was a sprig of rowan heavy with berries – the sign of the Badgerman. Steve turned the heavy iron handle. The door opened on to a short flight of steps leading down to the crypt. He felt around the wall for the light switch and flicked it on. The bulb flashed and went out with a faint ping. As he could see nothing he returned to the nave and walked along the aisle to the chancel, where, mumbling a garbled supplication for forgiveness, he took one of the tall processional candles from the altar. He found the matches under the hollow base of the brass candlestick.

When he had lit the candle he went back to the stairs, hot wax burning his hand. The crypt was longer and wider than he had imagined, but the ceiling lower. By candlelight it was possible to see all four walls indistinctly. It was a gloomy place to be interred. Better to be buried in the earth, thought Steve as he examined each tomb in turn, than to be encased in stone. Better to have spent the money on the poor. No one came down here any more.

Then there it was. He didn't see it until he had worked his way right round the vault. It was carved into the lid of a tomb which stood against the wall where he had come in. There was a sprig of rowan clasped in the stone hands of a forgotten country squire as he lay on top of his tomb all dressed up in armour.

Steve propped up the candle by the door and put all his effort into trying to raise the lid, but it might as well have been cemented down. Not to be put off, he bent down to examine the end of the tomb nearest the stairs. When he pushed, the panel grated backwards, allowing him a way in. He was relieved to discover that the tomb was empty.

When he crawled inside, the candle flickered, just enough to indicate a breeze. But the air outside in the crypt had been still. Steve shielded the candle with his body in case he had been mistaken, but the flame continued to gutter. Three sides of the tomb were made up by stone slabs, the fourth was formed by the wall of the church.

Inside the tomb, holding the flame close to the church wall, he began to inspect the stonework. Half-way through his search the flame began to flutter wildly like a loose flapping sail. When he cupped it in his hand it settled. There was no mortar between the stones in this area of the tomb and Steve could tell that behind them there was a hollow space.

He set the candle down and began to remove the stones. As soon as he had created an opening he re-sealed the tomb by pushing the panel back into place, and crawled through the wall. He found himself in a low tunnel about four feet square. The roof was supported by rough branches of oak, bristling with twigs. This was not a cave, or a mine, it was an underground wood. Steve rebuilt the wall of the crypt as best he could and set off down the gently sloping path, stooping as he went.

Just as the tunnel was becoming airless, it broadened out into a rocky space and there was room to stand up. He was in a limestone cavern. Tunnels ran off to right and left. Water dripped overhead. Steve shielded the candle from the cold breeze which blew down from a hidden opening in Rising Wood above. Then he crossed the cavern and entered the passage directly opposite. There were further turns and then the tunnel forked. If he made a mistake he might never find his way back. He stepped into the left fork. That way led downwards. He held the candle above his head. The flame flickered, but not much. He repeated the test in the second fork. The flame spluttered and nearly went out. He listened and sniffed, then returned to the passage on the left. He breathed deep. The air was musty, like wet leaves blocking a drain. That way lay earth. He decided to take the downward path, regardless of the fact that the right-hand one led towards the sky.

Before long the tunnel narrowed and then it moved upwards into a bottle-neck until Steve was forced to crawl on his hands and knees. He could go no further. At first, he thought he had come to a dead end, but then he discovered an opening in the ceiling. He shone the candle into the small space above. Had he been wrong in his choice after all? There seemed to be some kind of S bend ahead, dug out of the earth, taking the tunnel upwards to a higher level. If he was to go through at all, he would have to put the candle out. If he got stuck half-way, he would die a slow death by starvation. If he went back to St Thomas's he could sit it out and let things happen just as they always had.

What had Gem chanted in the wood?

> Bogwitch, Bogwitch,
> fills a need.
> Climb the ridge
> and plant your seed.

And before that?

> Bogwitch, Bogwitch,
> filled with greed.
> Dig for her
> and we'll be freed.

Steve extinguished the flame and squeezed into the opening. The S bend had been designed to accommodate a larger body, but even so his contortions made his back ache.

As he inched through the tunnel, clawing with his free hand, gripping with his knees and pushing upwards with his feet, he repeated the skipping songs syllable by agonizing syllable.

Then at last his head emerged into the cool darkness of another stretch of underground wood. The passageways were without doubt the work of the Badgerman.

Steve re-lit the candle and hurried on until he came to a low stone archway, about two feet high. He crawled through it and found himself in a stone-lined tunnel. After about five yards he emerged into a cavity. He guessed he was under the tower of St Peter's, close to the arch with the Badgerman's carving of rowan berries on it. Above him was a flagstone supported by a stout wooden frame. He pushed up hard and clambered out into the porch.

'What on earth has happened to you?' said Mrs Price when she opened the front door. 'Has the rugby season started early or something?'

Steve hadn't given his appearance much thought. The odd looks he'd received as he made his way from the church hadn't registered. Right now, he had other things on his mind.

'Is Pricey in?' he asked.

'No, he went up to see you a quarter of an hour ago. He borrowed your bike.'

It was half-past eight.

'I thought I'd call in to see if I could have my pendant back before I went home,' he said. 'I've decided to show it to my mum.'

Mrs Price looked at Steve doubtfully.

'I guess you've heard about her leaving.'

'Not heard,' said Mrs Price, kindly. 'It didn't take much to work it out for myself. You'd better come in for a minute.'

Steve was anxious to bring the subject back to the pendant, but in fact Mrs Price hadn't forgotten.

'I'll just pop upstairs and get it for you. Then if you're lucky you might run into David on your way home.'

She was gone longer than Steve expected, and when she returned to the kitchen she was pale.

'I don't know what to say,' she said. 'It was there this morning. At the bottom of my jewellery box. I saw it!'

Steve wanted to scream at her.

'I'll have another look,' she said. 'Perhaps I moved it. It was all so hectic this morning.'

Mrs Price went upstairs again. Before she came back down Pricey returned.

'There you are!' he said, hot and flustered from his anxious ride home. 'Thank God for that. What happened to you? You look wrecked!'

'We all are,' said Steve.

'What do you mean?'

'The pendant. It's gone. Your mum can't find it.'

'So?'

'That's what all the trouble's about. The Bogwitch is after it. It wasn't my bike she was after at all. It was what she thought I might have hidden in it.'

'But what does she want it for?'

'The rhyme. *Plant a seed and set us free*. The acorn must have something to do with it. And it looks like she's got it.'

'Last night?'

'No, they were still after it this afternoon when they caught up with me in the woods.'

'So what happened?'

Steve couldn't tell him, because Mrs Price had appeared in the doorway.

'It's definitely not there,' she said. 'I'm sorry. David, did you see Monica on your way back? She ought to be in by now.'

'Monica!' Pricey exclaimed, pushing back his seat. 'The little thief! I bet she's got it. She's always poking into other people's stuff.'

'Have you seen her?' said Mrs Price.

Pricey shook his head.

'We'd better look for her,' said Steve quietly.

'I'll check her room,' said Mrs Price, 'just in case she's left it on her dressing table.'

'No chance,' said Pricey, harshly. 'Let's go!'

The street was empty.

'Where do you think she is?' asked Steve.

'Best try the rec., and work back from there.'

The recreation ground lay on the slope of the hill on the southern edge of Ramswold. It was too steep for a decent game of football, but perfect for idling away the day free from prying adult eyes. While they hurried there Steve filled Pricey in on the events of the afternoon.

'Rather you than me,' said Pricey when he'd finished. 'I'd have just stayed put and waited to be rescued.'

'Yes,' said Steve, 'and you'd probably still be there.'

When they turned into the lane leading to the recreation ground they saw Monica hurrying towards them. She looked guilty; she knew she was late.

'You shouldn't be walking back on your own,' Pricey scolded. 'Where's Carol and Rachel? Mum will have a fit when I tell her.'

'Better not say anything then,' she jibed.

Pricey raised his hand to clip her behind the ear. Steve held him back.

'Where's Carol and Rachel?' he said.

'Gone home ages.' She was more willing to talk to Steve.

'Who've you been with?' said Pricey.

'No one. Been on my own.'

'Scared to come home!'

'Has anyone else talked to you?' asked Steve, anxious to put an end to their rowing. 'Any kids on bikes?'

'No,' said Monica, 'only a woman from the council, but that was when I was with Carol and Rachel. She was doing a survey of the field. She said they wanted to flatten it or something.'

'Level it, idiot,' said Pricey.

'Blonde woman. Hair like candyfloss?' asked Steve, but he needn't have bothered.

Monica nodded, unable to conceal another guilty look.

106

'Is she still there?' asked Pricey.

'Went off ages ago,' said Monica. 'Let's go. Mum's going to kill me as it is.'

'If we don't kill you first,' said Pricey, pulling her roughly in the direction of home, 'and you'll probably thank us for doing it because Mum's mad as hell because you've been in her things!'

'I haven't!' She began to punch and kick at Pricey, who had to loosen his grip on her to dodge her blows.

'Calm down Monica,' said Steve more kindly. Pricey's rough handling wouldn't get them anywhere. 'Have you seen my pendant? That's all I want to know. Your mum was looking after it for me.'

Monica began to cry. 'I didn't know,' she wailed, her face red with angry tears. 'I didn't know it was yours. I wouldn't have borrowed it if I'd known.'

'Flaming lost it,' said Pricey bitterly.

'Lay off, Pricey,' said Steve. 'That won't help.'

Pricey kicked a stone across the road and stuck his hand in his pockets to prevent himself from tearing his sister's head off. He bit his lip hard and spat into the dust.

'Where is it, Monica?' said Steve.

'Sold it. Carol said I should. *And* Rachel asked for more money. I didn't have any choice. She said she'd pay anything we asked!'

'How much?' said Pricey.

'Twenty pounds for me and five each for Carol and Rachel. She said that her daughter was called Gem. She said she wanted it as a present. I didn't know it was yours, Steve. She made me sell it! I thought it was one of Mum's old ones that she didn't wear any more because it was right at the bottom with all the junky stuff I used to wear when I was little and I dressed up.'

'Idiot!' shouted Pricey. 'Since when has Mum been called Gem?'

Steve swore loudly, but it wasn't Monica's fault. How had the Bogwitch known where to find the pendant? Was it just coincidence that she had encountered Monica or had she somehow engineered the whole situation?

'When did you take it, Monica?' he said. 'If you give me an honest answer Pricey won't shout at you any more.'

'After tea,' she said, 'when Mum and David were washing up. I don't know why I did it. I just wanted to wear something different to show Rachel and Carol. I wish I hadn't. I'm sorry, Steve, I really am!'

Was that how the Bogwitch worked? By exploiting people's weaknesses?

'Monica,' said Steve as they turned back on to the High Street, 'I'll tell your mum that you've given it back to me.'

'What?' said Pricey.

'I have got this, though,' said Monica, butting in again. She had taken a twenty pound note from her pocket.

'I don't want the money,' said Steve.

'I didn't mean the money, but you can have it if you want. Maybe you could buy it back?'

Steve smiled. He would hate to disillusion her.

'I meant this,' Monica continued. She had unfolded the twenty pound note to reveal what had been wrapped up inside.

'What is it?' said Steve. It was a stupid question. He could see perfectly well that it was a shrivelled brown acorn.

'It was inside the pendant.'

'What?' said Steve.

'I was fiddling with it and by accident I unscrewed the nut from the cup. It was inside. I took it out and screwed the nut back. I was going to put it back inside later, but when I tried to unscrew the nut bit again, it wouldn't budge. So I just shoved the acorn into my pocket.'

'Blimey,' said Pricey.

'Monica,' said Steve, 'you are wonderful with a capital W!' He picked her up and hugged her. She blushed and squirmed away. She didn't understand this about-turn in her fortunes, and Steve wasn't going to explain. 'You keep the twenty quid, and I'll have the acorn! Did you tell the woman about it?'

'No, I didn't think she'd pay up if she knew a bit was missing. I just kept quiet.'

Steve could have hugged her again but, in deference to Pricey, restrained himself.

Monica yawned. She was tired. Pricey ushered her on ahead.

'What *is* going on?' asked Pricey when she was out of earshot.

'This,' said Steve, rolling the acorn around in his palm, 'is what the Bogwitch is really after. Let's hope she doesn't know it!'

'The pendant was just another place to hide it then?'

'Seems like it,' Steve agreed.

'But what's so important about a mouldy old acorn, then?'

'I'm not sure, exactly,' said Steve, 'but I think it's about time we found the Badgerman.'

'How can we?' said Pricey. 'My mum said he'd gone away, or at least her great-grandmother did.'

'He might have come back. Think about it. Where was Gem going the night she died? I mean, after she chucked her bike into the Cauldron.'

'If she did.'

'I'm sure she did.'

'But the water?'

'There are a lot of things we don't know about, Pricey. This time last week did you believe in the Bogwitch?'

'No.'

'Do you now?'

'Yes, I think so.'

'And the Badgerman?'

'Maybe.'

'I do! Now, listen. The acorn is important, right?'

Pricey nodded.

'Gem was given it by her father, who according to Mrs Titmarsh was someone local. The Bogwitch wants the acorn. Why? Because Gem was trying to do something with it the night she died, and if the Bogwitch gets the acorn, then that thing can never be done, unless of course she wants to do it herself. Gem told me what she was trying to do when she sang to me in the wood, didn't she?

> Bogwitch, Bogwitch,
> fills a need.
> Climb the ridge
> and plant your seed.

'The acorn. She was trying to plant it.'

'But why, Steve?'

'Dunno, to get rid of the Bogwitch maybe. We must find the Badgerman. Use your brains, Pricey. At a small family funeral, who would you expect to be there?'

'Parents, brothers, sisters, grandparents, uncles, very close friends.'

'What was that first one?'

Pricey was growing impatient. 'Mum and Dad.'

'Don't you see? Mum, grandparents, some school-friends, Mrs Titmarsh, who was a sort of adopted aunt . . .'

'And this Mr Brockworth. Her father! Steve, he could be her father!'

110

'Exactly, and he has the same initial as the forester in the church guidebook.'

'You mean, he's the same.'

'Mr Brockworth is the Badgerman, I'm sure of it, and that's where Gem was heading that night. She was going to see the Badgerman.'

'Her father?'

'Yes. This acorn, the one the Bogwitch wants so badly, belongs to the Badgerman. And we must return it, so we can learn what has to be done.'

'Us?' said Pricey, sitting down wearily on a fire hydrant.

'We must find him tomorrow.'

'Can't,' said Pricey. 'We're going on holiday on Friday evening remember. I've got to go to Mill Bottom with Mum to get some new T-shirts and stuff.'

'Friday then?'

'Can't. I've got to help clean the house and pack, and then there's my music lesson.'

'Can't you sneak out for a while?'

'I don't know,' said Pricey, 'I really don't know.'

Was Pricey raising objections because he didn't want to face up to what was happening? Steve began to suspect as much but he didn't want to push it. After all, he was afraid too.

13

Steve knew his father was going to be furious with him for being late. But things were far worse than he could have imagined. The Bogwitch was sitting in the kitchen when he got home. Worse still, his father couldn't see her for what she really was. Gardenia was sitting in his mother's place at the table, smoking a cigarette. Not even his father had been allowed to do that in the house. Two dog-ends lay crumpled in her saucer and the table was flecked with ash. Her tea-cup – his mother's best china – was smudged with lipstick.

'And where may I ask have you been?' said Mr Armstrong. 'Just look at the state of you!'

Steve said nothing.

'And do you know who this is?' Mr Armstrong continued, indicating the woman with the beehive. He didn't wait for Steve to answer. 'Mrs Savage, the Mayor of Ramswold, and she tells me that you've been into her garden while she was out and vandalized her garage roof!'

Steve remained silent. Avoiding his father's eyes, he gazed impassively at the Bogwitch. He locked her out of his thoughts. She was so smug and confident now that she had what she imagined to be her prize. What was she doing here? Whatever, he wasn't going to let her see the truth Gem had planted inside his head back in June. The true acorn would remain safe with him.

'What have you got to say for yourself?' asked Mr Armstrong.

The Bogwitch opened her handbag and took out her compact, allowing Steve a glimpse of the pendant wedged between her purse and cheque book. When it became obvious that Steve was not going to speak, she said: 'Well, in that case, Mr Armstrong, I wonder if you would mind accompanying me back to my house with the boy? We shall see if confronting him with the damage can jog his memory. I would hate to call the police. I just don't understand what your son has got against me.'

What was the point of going back to her house now? There could only be danger there. The car would be gone from the ice house and so would the festering badger pelts.

'All right,' Steve said. 'So I tore a few tiles off her roof. I don't know why I did it. I'm just fed up with everything. Satisfied?'

'I am not!' shouted Mr Armstrong. 'Take it out on me or our own house by all means – and that would be bad enough – but why pick on Mrs Savage, a woman living all on her own?'

'I don't know,' said Steve, adopting a confused tone. 'I happened to be there, that's all. By accident. It could have happened anywhere.'

Was the Bogwitch enjoying it? Steve couldn't tell. Now she had the chance to show just how magnanimous she was.

'I *am* sorry, Mr Armstrong, I hadn't realized that Stephen was under an emotional strain. It can be so difficult for young people these days.'

And whose fault is that? thought Steve.

'It's not you who should apologize, Mrs Savage,' said Mr Armstrong. 'What have you got to say for yourself, Steve?'

Insincerity was the preferred weapon of the moment. 'I'm sorry, Mrs Savage,' he said. 'I'm very sorry indeed.'

'I shall come down with Stephen first thing tomorrow, Mrs Savage,' said Mr Armstrong, 'and repair your roof.'

113

'No, no, Mr Armstrong, there's no need for that. I've got the builders coming back to make one or two finishing touches to the house anyway, so I'll get them to see to it. You'd be better off using your time to take Stephen to the doctor's. He obviously needs help.'

Mr Armstrong bit his lip and glared at Steve.

'Now,' said the woman with the beehive, 'could I just use your loo before I go?'

'Of course,' said Mr Armstrong. Steve hated to see his father so deferential. 'Upstairs, the door on the right.'

Instead of putting her cigarette out, the Bogwitch walked towards the stairs with the stub still glued to her bottom lip.

Mr Armstrong turned to Steve when she had left the room. 'Well?' he said. 'Have you really sunk to this?'

Steve was going to say, 'It's not my fault!' but that course lacked dignity. He had attacked the roof on purpose, he had felt all the hate and frustration which he had just expressed. He still did. The only difference was that he had not explained the real reason for it. He had nothing to be ashamed of.

'If it's OK with you, I'll have a bath when she's gone,' he said.

Mr Armstrong nodded. 'And then to bed early. I'm sure things will look different in the morning. I'm off out for a drink with Monk in a minute. I'll see you tomorrow. We can have a talk then if you feel like it.'

Soaking in a hot bath proved to be anything but soothing. Not even the steam could dispel the smell of Bogwitch's cigarette from the room, and opening the window didn't help. The evening was airless.

Steve dried himself off and drained the bath, leaving an earthy ring around the high-water mark, then retreated to his brother's bed under the attic window. The dusk outside stank of hot tar and the bitterness of summer bonfires.

114

Gem's rowan sprig had withered and died. His father had thrown it out, and the Bogwitch had invaded the house.

Eventually, Steve slipped into a breathless, red-eyed sleep. At about one o'clock he woke again, from a dream of forest fires. Smoke was curling up between the floorboards, clearly visible in the moonlight. His eyes streamed. He opened the window and hung his head out to catch a breath of fresh air. An orange light danced across the bank below. The bathroom was on fire.

Steve threw off his duvet and struggled into his jeans. Then he crossed the room and flung open the door. Smoke billowed in from the stairs. Slamming the door shut, he raced back to his bed, grabbed the acorn from under his pillow and shoved it into his pocket. Then he shouted and stamped on the floor to rouse his father.

When this brought no response, he wrapped his T-shirt round his face, took a deep breath, opened his door and groped his way down the smoke-filled staircase. He could see little when he reached the landing, but enough to realize that the bathroom door was shut. He tried to turn on the light, but the wiring had gone.

He felt his way around the landing to his father's room. He opened the door and went in. The smoke was less dense than on the landing, but the heavy velvet curtains drawn across the window made it impossible to see. He called out. But again there was no response.

Afraid, he fumbled his way round the side of the bed. He grabbed the duvet where he imagined his father would be and shook it. The bed had not been slept in. Surely his father couldn't have fallen asleep in the bath when he came in from the pub? No, he would still be at Monk's house, talking into the night.

He hurried back to the door. As he was about to step out on to the landing, the bathroom burst open and a wave of

115

flame rolled across the carpet and broke up against the attic stairs, then rolled down the steps towards the kitchen. Steve slammed the door behind him as flames began to lick the edge of the bedroom carpet. He tore back the heavy curtains and opened the window. The inrush of air fanned the flames and the door began to ripple with fire. The wallpaper caught and the ceiling blackened. As Steve jumped, his father's duvet flared up like a torch. And as he crash-landed half on and half off the porch the fire tore a hole in the roof overhead and slates exploded skywards.

Steve dropped down to the yard, and was on his bike in seconds. Instead of racing down the hill to rouse his neighbours, he turned left round the side of the house and pushed the bike up the bank into the wood. From the shelter of the trees he watched the cottage roof collapse and heard the alarm being raised.

As the fire consumed the cottage, spreading light through the fringe of the wood, Steve eased himself back until he could no longer feel the heat on his bare chest. He put his T-shirt on. It was time to disappear, time to find the Badgerman. It couldn't wait. If the Bogwitch realized that he had survived the fire, she would make another attempt on his life and sooner or later she would succeed.

But what of his family? Perhaps his going would bring them back together. And Pricey? They would take another photograph next year. Pricey would be all right. They would all be OK if he could find the Badgerman and do for the Bogwitch.

Steve turned his back on the fire and rode away fast without lights. As his wheels hummed along the top path he began to feel disembodied, and he passed like a ghost under the trees. He didn't stop until he came to the platform of rock above High Force. Behind him the night sky glowed orange. The fire had caught a hold in Rising Wood.

Steve pushed his bike upstream until he reached a point where he could cross, then turned down the opposite bank. From there he made his way along the Oakridge, and dropped down the far side to pick up the cycle path on the outskirts of Mill Bottom. When he reached the old railway bridge across the Wood Spring he dismounted, rolled up his jeans and manoeuvred the bike down the embankment into the stream. Only twenty yards distant was the spot where Gem had tried to cross the main road on the night she died.

When Steve had followed the stream under the road bridge he dragged his bike back up the bank on the other side. He found himself on the edge of a rough paddock. The grass was long and spiked with thistles. To each side of him stood a line of trees of uniform height, their branches intertwining above his head. They were unmistakably rowans.

Beyond the paddock was a cottage set well back from the road. All he could see of it was the dark shape of its gable end. Steve crossed the grass to the cobbled yard at the back of the cottage. There was no sign of life. An ancient Foden tow truck, with lifting gear mounted on its flat-bed, stood in the far corner. The front nearside tyre was flat. A green Land Rover with a soft back was parked in front of it. The canopy was ragged. The windscreen was smeared with muck. It didn't look as if it had been used for a long time.

Steve was tired and cold. The orange glow on the horizon above Rising Wood was fading. The fire was being brought under control. When Steve rattled the back door there was no response. And it was the same at the front. But his disappointment was short-lived. There, above the door, carved in relief on the stone lintel, was a sprig of rowan heavy with berries.

14

When Steve woke up in the back of the Land Rover, where he had made himself comfortable under some old sacks, the sun had already begun to rise. He climbed down to the cobbled yard and stretched.

The cottage looked smaller in daylight, but no less deserted. There was a mountain of logs behind the Foden which he hadn't noticed the night before and a rusty pump just beyond the back door. A collection of ramshackle sheds lay some distance away on the other side of the Land Rover with their backs turned to the wood. A goat chewed grass at the end of its chain. Chickens scratched unheeding around its feet.

So, he thought, this is what it's like to be dead. At that very moment his family would be mourning his death. If he had not died in the cottage, then surely they would think he must have perished in the woods?

Steve tried the back door again. He knocked twice, and rattled the handle. It was locked tight. Spiders had colonized the kitchen window, spinning their sticky nests in every crack and crevice. The glass was as grimy as the Land Rover's, making it impossible to see in.

Steve gave up on the back door and fetched some sacking from the Land Rover to wrap around his shoulders. Then he walked round to the front of the cottage.

The cottage was set in a large plot of land bordered by mountain ash trees on all sides. It was from these trees that the house took its name, Rowan Cottage. A vegetable patch lay between the drive and the front path. It was sadly neglected. A wisp of blue smoke curled up from a squat chimney set in the angle of the low roof.

Steve banged on the front door. When there was no response he knocked again.

He had just turned away, when the latch cracked like a gun and the door was flung open. He stopped with a start and spun round. His first glimpse of the figure towering in the doorway filled him with panic. He wanted to run, but there was nowhere to go. The man fixed him with one bloodshot eye. The other was half closed, as if permanently squinting into the sun. It was totally blind. Its once youthful brown had faded to the colour of ash. Steve was unable to move.

The man was old, in his late sixties by the look of him, but he was powerfully built. His hands were large and calloused, his arms heavily veined, his muscles still taut. The grey stubble of several days' growth shadowed his sharp cheek bones and bristled from his chin. His pale blue work shirt was dirty at the collar and creased, as were his heavy woollen trousers. His white hair was dishevelled. Steve guessed he had slept in his clothes. He smelled sourly of strong drink.

'Mr Brockworth?' said Steve, suddenly conscious that he didn't look much better himself.

The old man said nothing. Instead he raised his hand to support himself against the heavy stone lintel and eyed Steve's bare feet and the sacks which were beginning to slip from his shoulders.

'I'm looking for Mr Brockworth,' said Steve, as if repetition of the name were the only way to make progress.

When the man spoke, his tone was irritable. All he said was: 'Who?'

'Mr Brockworth.'

'And who's he when he's at home?'

Had he after all come to the wrong place?

'Gem's father. The Badgerman!'

The old man sniffed loudly and looked at Steve, his one eye wild and flickering. 'I don't know you or what you're talking about, coming here to disturb me, all ragged and stinking of fire.' Then he broke off, looking past Steve's shoulder to the rowans by the gate. 'Stopped doing your job properly, have you?' he bellowed. 'Things that bad, are they? What have you let through to plague me? A tortured wraith? Vandal? A cruel arsonist who'd set the woods alight with a box of stolen matches and a jam jar full of petrol, and damn everything that lives and grows in it?' Then he turned to Steve, his whole body shaking. 'Now be off back to where you came from, before I lose my temper!'

The door slammed shut as suddenly as it had opened, and Steve heard the man's heavy boots retreat down the hall. He thumped on the door again. When he got no reply he peered through the window. The man was hunched over a stout deal table. Steve rapped on the glass. The old man raised a white porcelain mug to his lips and drained the contents, then refilled it from a demijohn resting in his lap.

Steve returned to the front door, and shouted through the letter box: 'You've got to let me in! I've got nowhere else to go.' Then he screamed, 'The Bogwitch tried to kill me last night. She burnt my house down!' He pounded the door with his fists until the hinges rattled. 'Rise Cottage, where Gem used to live,' and then he added for good measure: 'The Bogwitch set fire to Rising Wood. You are Mr Brockworth, aren't you? You've got to be! If you aren't, then it's too late for all of us!'

He allowed the flap of the letterbox to snap back into place and sat down exhausted in the porch, breathing heavily, with his back against the door. The shock of recent events threatened to overwhelm him.

Ten minutes passed before he heard footsteps returning down the hall. He was half-way to his feet when the door was flung open.

'What you say?' said the old man. 'Do you want the whole world to hear it?' He tripped on the mat and fell forward like a great tree. Steve caught him in the chest and shouldered him back up against the door jamb.

'I said, "Are you Mr Brockworth?" '

'What if I am?'

'Then you *are* the Badgerman?'

The old man wiped his mouth with the back of his hand, and then looked at it with disgust. 'I was,' he said bitterly, 'and on good days sometimes I think I still am. Today is not a good day. So, if you're from the Bogwitch, be gone before I get my hands to your scrawny neck. If not, you must speak and be quick about it.'

'Gem came to me with a message. On Midsummer's Eve,' said Steve. 'It took a long time to work out. She led me to this.' He took the acorn from his pocket. 'I thought you might know what she wants me to do with it?'

The old man snatched it from his hand and held it up to the light, squinting at it through his drunken eye.

'I can't tell, I can't tell,' he said in frustration, 'it's so long since I've seen it. It looks more withered. Where did you find it?'

He slipped it into his trouser pocket. Steve wanted to protest, but instead he said: 'Inside Gem's silver pendant, hidden in the frame of her bike. I found her bike in the Cauldron.'

'Cauldron?' said the Badgerman, suspiciously.

'The pool below High Force.'

'No wonder it's survived, then,' said the Badgerman,

distractedly. 'She sank it in All's Well for safe-keeping. *That* was what she was coming back to tell me!'

'All's Well?' said Steve.

'Below High Force,' snapped the Badgerman. 'Don't you know the pool is called All's Well? Or at least it was in the old days . . .'

'Before the Bogwitch came back?' said Steve.

The Badgerman nodded, but his thoughts had once again flown elsewhere. When he spoke, his voice was still gruff, but his tone was much less hostile.

'Better come in then,' he said. 'The doorstep is no place to talk.'

Steve found himself being tugged into the low, oak-panelled hall. The flagstone floor was caked with dry mud. Dead leaves had been carried in through the front door and blown into the corners. They had never been swept up.

'You say she set fire to the wood last night? I thought I smelled it when I woke this morning.'

'*And* my house,' said Steve.

'That's bad,' the Badgerman agreed. 'How could I have slept through it? Where did you sleep? The back of the Land Rover? You should have knocked!'

'I did,' said Steve.

'And I didn't hear? Perhaps that was a good thing,' said the Badgerman, clapping his hand around Steve's shoulder. 'I was worse for wear last night, and would probably have torn your head right off. And then where would we be?'

And where were they? Steve wondered. The old man's initial aggression, barely tempered now by his attempt to be reasonable, made Steve wary. He was relieved when the weight of the Badgerman's hand was lifted from his shoulder.

The Badgerman led Steve down the hall, past the open door of a dusty parlour on the left, then ducked through a doorway to his right, and down a worn stone step into the kitchen.

He bent down to riddle the stove. 'Damn thing,' he muttered. Then he stood up and busied himself with the kettle. 'You'll want tea, I suppose?'

The Badgerman was not what he'd expected. He was not the kind of person the Church would want to depict in a stained glass window in this day and age. Perhaps he never had been.

'Sit down, sit down,' said the Badgerman. 'What are you waiting for?'

A dismantled chainsaw lay on the table and an assortment of parts littered every chair but one. When Steve still hesitated, the Badgerman grew exasperated.

'For God's sake, are you blind, boy?' he said. 'Have mine. And while you're about it, see that old pullover in the corner? Put it on before you catch your death.'

Steve did as he was told and sat down.

'Like rabbit and mushrooms, do you?' asked the Badgerman.

He held up four strips of pink meat.

Steve hesitated.

'One piece or two?'

'Two, please,' said Steve.

He watched as the Badgerman lumbered unsteadily about the kitchen fetching what he needed.

'What's your name then?' he said at last, bending down to peer into the stove.

'Stephen Armstrong.'

'Pour us another drink then, Stephen,' he said.

With some reluctance, Steve did as he was told.

When the Badgerman had drained his mug of wine, he began to make breakfast.

His hands shook as he cranked, riddled and cursed the

123

range into surrendering its heat. Then, when he had swept the chainsaw to one end of the table with his forearm and cleared another seat, he served the meal and set the teapot down with a crash.

'Now, eat!' he said.

The rabbit was burnt and blackened, but heady with the aroma of meadow mushrooms. Steve was hesitant at first, but seeing that the Badgerman ate voraciously, stabbing the meat with his fork, he soon followed suit, and swilled down each mouthful with great gulps of tea made with goat's milk.

When they had finished, the Badgerman pushed aside his empty demijohn and reached for the teapot. The food had calmed him for a little while.

'Tell me about Gem, then. That's why you've come, isn't it?'

Steve attempted to put his tired thoughts into some kind of order. After several false starts, he began to tell his tale in earnest. By the time he had finished the Badgerman had grown pale, his voice barely controlled.

'So you think that because you've found me, there's still hope?' he said. And then added, wearily, 'Well, I'm sorry to disillusion you, but as you can see, I've given up the fight.'

'You can't,' said Steve.

The Badgerman swept his arm across the table, sending plates and cutlery crashing to the floor.

'Who are you to come here telling me what to do?' he bellowed. He stood up abruptly, lurched backwards into his chair and staggered over to the stove. He stood with his hands on the hot rail, his back to the table, shoulders shaking with rage. Without taking his eyes from the old man's back, Steve fumbled around on the floor for his fallen table knife, but before he could find it, the Badgerman gave the fire-box door a vicious kick and rounded on him.

'Can't give up!' shouted the Badgerman. 'What do you

mean, *can't*? I already have. Ever since I sent my own daughter out to face that vile aberration of a woman thirty years ago. Gem was half me and half of humankind, so what hope do you think you've got? I, the Badgerman, can't venture beyond my ring of trees for fear of being destroyed by her. And how long do you think the rowans will keep her out? She does what she wants. It's too late. Forget about Ramswold, Stephen. It's doomed.'

The Badgerman kicked the catch of the fire-box door. It swung open, revealing the fire within.

'See this?' he said, taking the acorn from his pocket. 'Shall I throw it in? Do you really want to see the Valley Bottom Badger? Do you believe in her? Would you even have the courage to look upon her if you woke her from her long sleep? Because that is what you'd have to do if you wanted to rid Ramswold of the Bogwitch. You're nothing, Stephen Armstrong. You've come across me through lucky chance. Your mistake was to wake up when Gem came into your yard. Shall I burn the last acorn of the first oak to rise at the entrance to this pathetic little valley? Shall I?'

The Badgerman moved his hand closer to the flames. Steve thought of his family, of Pricey, of Monica, Henry Gray. The others, the tortured wraiths, and Gem who had come to him to tell him about what must be done. As the Badgerman plunged his hand into the fire, Steve pushed back his chair and leapt across the table. He tore at the Badgerman's arm and pulled his hand out of the flames. The great man toppled drunkenly and fell, pushing Steve down against the table. The Badgerman rolled over on the floor and lay there semi-conscious, eye closed, his hand unmarked by the furnace.

Steve shuffled over to where the Badgerman had fallen and prised open his huge fist. The acorn was unharmed. The old man began to stir. Steve slipped the acorn into his

125

pocket and stood up. He looked down at the Badgerman, sprawled across the filthy kitchen floor.

'I've come this far,' he shouted. 'I'll work it out for myself.' Then he added, cruelly, 'If you no longer care about your daughter, I do!'

The Badgerman propped himself up on one elbow and shook his head fiercely. Steve turned towards the hall. But he stopped when he reached the door. He knew there was nothing to be gained by leaving. He sat down wearily on the step and watched as the old man struggled to his feet.

'The acorn was inside my fist,' said the Badgerman, and then added quietly, 'Fire cannot harm me. I was born of it.'

He shuffled over to his chair and sat down, resting his head on the table. Before Steve could get up, he had fallen asleep.

15

Afraid to remain in the kitchen with the slumbering Badgerman, Steve hid himself in the Land Rover until the late afternoon, by which time he felt the old man must be sober. It was with trepidation that he returned to the cottage to put the kettle on. His feeling of foreboding deepened when he discovered that the stove had gone out. The Badgerman began to stir.

'Still here,' he grunted, when he opened his eye. He rubbed his chin and reached for his demijohn, but it was empty.

'I have nowhere else to go,' said Steve, and then added after a pause. 'Everyone thinks I'm dead.'

'Better keep it that way then,' said the Badgerman. 'The Bogwitch can't see you behind the rowans. Stay if you want.'

It was what Steve had wanted to hear, but he wished it had been said with more enthusiasm.

'You seem to be hoping for some sign that the world can be put right again,' continued the Badgerman, 'but not much in this life is certain. However, you can guarantee that a fire will die if you don't feed it. You've let the stove go out.'

'I'm sorry,' said Steve, 'I didn't know . . .'

'. . . that you were meant to keep it in,' continued the Badgerman. 'No matter. What's done is done.'

He rose up unsteadily from his chair and cast a disparaging eye over the kitchen. 'God what a mess!' he said. 'I suppose it's time I put the chainsaw back together.' Then he addressed Steve directly. 'And you, as you insist on staying, might as well make yourself useful. There's wood to chop for the fire.'

The Badgerman crossed the room and rested his hand on Steve's shoulder. 'The axe is in the parlour under the sofa,' he said.

Steve looked up at the Badgerman. Now was not the moment for conversation.

When Steve unwrapped the neat folds of oil-cloth which protected the axe, he marvelled at the gleaming steel head, seamlessly joined to the shaft of polished oak. When he drew his thumb over the blade, blood welled up from the cut. He sucked his thumb hard and the bleeding stopped.

The axe was finely balanced. It felt light in his hands. The prospect of using it suddenly thrilled him, and he smiled for the first time since he'd hugged Monica the day before.

On his return to the kitchen, Steve saw that the Badgerman had opened another demijohn of wine. He looked up from his mug and said: 'There's thick socks and old work boots by the door. Put them on. You can start on the log pile behind the tow truck.'

When Steve had been kitted out, he was ushered out of the door.

Because he had been given no advice about using the axe, it was two hours before he managed to split a log cleanly. Twice Steve returned to the cottage for help and found the doors locked. The Badgerman worked on his chainsaw and ignored all Steve's efforts to attract his attention.

Eventually, Steve became master of his task. Each time he swung the axe, it described a perfect, glistening arc through the dusk. And its languid *chock* became the natural accompaniment to the thrush which sang high up in the rowans on the edge of Whispering Wood.

When night fell, the Badgerman appeared at the back door, his head bowed under the lintel, his shoulders filling the frame.

'You can come in now,' he called, 'and make supper.'

'But I can't cook,' Steve protested, and sat down exhausted on the pile of logs he had chopped.

'And bring some wood in while you're about it,' shouted the Badgerman.

When Steve went in to refuel the stove, the Badgerman was making the final adjustments to his saw. The table was clean and the demijohn only a quarter empty. Then, turning to face Steve, the Badgerman jerked the chainsaw into life with a roar that threatened to tear the cottage apart. But it stopped as suddenly as it had begun, and the old man gestured that Steve should light the stove.

Supper was a crude affair: a few scraps of rabbit, burnt beyond recognition, and a mess of over-cooked vegetables. The Badgerman cast a scornful eye over his plate, but nevertheless ate a full helping and then asked for more. When he had finished, he sat back in his chair with hands behind his head. Steve began to gather up the plates.

'It's good to eat in company again,' said the Badgerman. 'You'll probably be surprised to hear it, but your cooking has done me the power of good.'

Steve turned quickly to the sink to hide his smile. Indeed he had noticed that some of the colour was returning to the old man's eye. When he had put the dirty plates on the draining board, he filled the kettle. The Badgerman poured himself another drink and said: 'Leave the dishes.'

'It's no trouble,' said Steve. 'It won't take a minute.'

'Since when has washing up been important?' growled the Badgerman. 'Seeing that you are determined to stay, we must talk. Forget about tea. Have a drink.'

'No thanks,' Steve replied, returning to his chair.

The Badgerman smiled, revealing a set of discoloured but otherwise perfect teeth.

'As you wish,' he said, and hammered the stopper back into the neck of the demijohn with his fist.

Steve studied the Badgerman across the table.

'Not many would dare look at the Badgerman so closely or for so long,' the old man observed. 'Ah, but I wasn't always so dishevelled. You've found me in a sorry state. I can't even look in the mirror any more. How old do you think I am? How old do you have to be to get like this?'

Steve tried to picture the stained glass in St Peter's and recall what had been written in the guidebook. He made a guess.

'Three hundred years?' he said.

The Badgerman laughed. 'You think of me as a mere sapling! I was already a man when the Romans came to the valley. But they didn't stay long, though they laid the foundations of a fairly useful road. The people were too wild for them and didn't take kindly to thinking in straight lines. But I wasn't the first Badgerman, Stephen. There were others before me, so long ago that I've forgotten their names. My memory comes and goes. Managing a wood and maintaining all those tunnels is hard and dirty work. You think chopping wood is difficult. That's like snapping dead twigs for kindling. I'm old and my four badgers have gone. Even the one who lives in Rising Wood has given up on me. For all I know, he may be dead like all the rest.'

Steve sat forward in his chair. His voice trembled as he spoke: 'Was he slightly lame?'

The old man brightened. 'You're telling me you've seen him? Where?'

'I must have been sitting above his sett.'

'Beneath a tall straight beech?'

130

Steve nodded. 'Sniper shot him. He was hit but he ran off. So fast that I had no hope of following him.'

The Badgerman uncorked his jar and topped up his mug. His one eye blazed as if once more he was trying to see his way through the darkness of the wood.

'He's wily,' he said, 'he'll have gone to ground to heal himself. What evil there is in the world! And not enough badgers left to seek it out. You've seen the ice house. There's no life after badgers, only darkness and chaos. A wood without a badger is a night without a moon. I have neglected my work!'

'There's still time,' said Steve.

'I should never have gone away,' continued the Badgerman, thumping the table so hard that his wine slopped over the brim of his mug. 'Do you love Ramswold, Stephen? Yes, I can see that you do. To you it is the world, and to me it was too, for so many long centuries, until I got bored with it. I began to yearn for foreign places. But what did I discover on my journey around the globe? Only what I already knew. There's nothing of importance to be found anywhere that could not be discovered in sleepy old Ramswold, if only you knew how to look! How could I have been so stupid? The ancient Ramswolders thought that the valley was a world in miniature. And they were right. The place has a significance beyond its size. *All's Well in Ramswold, all's Well in the world*. The Ramswold valley is a wonderful place. High Force sends its healing waters out through the mouth of the valley and adds to the well-being of the world. While Ramswold survives, the rest of the earth is in with a fighting chance!'

Steve remembered what it was like to be submerged like a trout on the bottom of the pool.

'That was why Gem hid her bicycle in All's Well,' he

said, 'that's why it was preserved! Why didn't you just go and retrieve it?'

'I couldn't see it, Stephen,' said the Badgerman, 'because the acorn was gone and I was blinded by grief. I just gave up.'

'Why couldn't you see without the acorn?'

'Patience,' said the Badgerman. 'Tomorrow I will show you. Have you still got it safe?'

Steve patted his trouser pocket. Then, realizing that he wasn't going to hear any more about the acorn, he got up to make a pot of tea.

When he returned to the table with a full mug, the Badgerman said: 'I must tell you about the Bogwitch. As far as Ramswold is concerned she is just a demon from the old legends. But she does exist, as you and your friend Pricey have discovered. In her time, she has had many names. When I sent Gem out on that fateful night she was known as Mrs Savage, and now she is Gardenia, too. She is insidious and poisonous. She's the gas in the badger setts, she's the hand that breaks the badger's jaw with the edge of a spade and lets the dogs loose to finish the job. At the moment she has fooled Ramswold into thinking that she is the soul of respectability, but she is twisted and evil. You say she is Mayor of Ramswold? Things have come to a pretty pass!'

'But where did she come from?' asked Steve.

'Where did any of us come from?' said the Badgerman. 'The Bogwitch has been around since there were men and women. But I could contain her in the damp places at the bottom of the valley. My badgers patrolled the hillsides and I worked on the woods to make them strong. A dark spirit is not happy amongst healthy trees. I tried to influence the people of the valley but, in the end, a Badgerman has no hold on men and women. In good and bad, human beings act alone.'

'But you defeated the Bogwitch,' said Steve, encouraging the old man to say more. 'Pricey's mum said so.'

'I thought that if I could get rid of her, I could get some peace. I thought that my work would be done and I could wander far from the valley . . .'

The Badgerman broke off and stood up to stoke the range. When he returned to the table, he cupped his hands around his mug. But he didn't drink. For a moment he fell completely silent.

Then he began again: 'About three hundred and fifty years ago, one Midsummer's Eve, the time of year when the Bogwitch was at her weakest, I took my axe down from the wall and called my four badgers. They summoned their clans from the four woods and we met in the quarry above the cottage. When darkness fell and we were sure that the valley slept, we set off through the tunnels, moving stealthily until we reached Boggarts Holm. There, we spread out deep beneath the ground, with the Bogwitch's cottage above. Then I thrust my axe up through the subsoil to the waterlogged turf, and unleashed a furious scrabbling of claws. Boggarts Holm erupted. The valley woke. But before anyone could reach their window to witness it, the Bogwitch's house had collapsed, and she herself had been dragged under the earth to be torn limb from limb.' The Badgerman spat into his mug. 'But her remains only poisoned the soil. I should have let the badgers take her to the Oakridge, where they could have cast her from the world. But even that would not have been an end of her. I know that now.'

'But I thought the Valley Bottom Badger was involved,' said Steve. 'What did she do?'

'She did nothing. She still slept on in her great sett under the hill. It is men who felt the need to invent her involvement that night. Stories change in the telling over the years. Sometimes I think they can never have a proper ending, and that's the way it was with the Bogwitch. When I thought she was gone I left on my travels, but as soon as I was abroad her spirit seeped from the earth and she became whole again. Without me to keep her in check she blighted the valley. When I returned, things were far worse than I could ever have imagined. She had been enslaving the dead and twisting their spirits to her own evil purposes.'

'Gem and the others, you mean?' said Steve.

The Badgerman clenched his fist. Steve thought the old man might lose control, but he held himself together.

'She would take someone with great potential just as they were about to leave childhood behind. Nathan Sawyer, the wood carver; Adam Hoggis, the cook; Thomas Smith, the gun maker; and Henry Gray, the artist. And my own Gem? What an athlete she was! By leaving a curse on every generation, the Bogwitch increased her strength.'

Steve sipped at his tea nervously, but it had long since grown cold.

'And where did she lock up their spirits,' continued the Badgerman, 'so that she could summon them as she wished? In the ice house, among the festering pelts. Those poor tormented souls are sent abroad in the night to inflict terrible damage. They engineer quarrels. They sow doubt and darkness in children's dreams. And, most evil of all, she makes those poor, enslaved spirits corporeal. She gives them back their bodies so that she can torture them further.'

'But there's still some good left in them,' said Steve. 'I've seen it in Henry's Gray's drawing and I sensed it in Adam Hoggis. And in Gem, especially Gem.'

'Oh, Gem,' sighed the Badgerman, 'if only she could have come here at midsummer when spirits wander free, I might have been able to help her. But she was tied to her home at Rise Cottage. She never lived here. When she abandoned the bicycle to the pool, she must have realized she couldn't succeed in her task. She knew she was going to die. I despair. She who was most strong and good has become the most twisted of all. Her loss has doubled the Bogwitch's power.'

The Badgerman began to talk rapidly, reliving the past. 'When I came back to the valley, I realized the mistake I had made. I had tried to rid Ramswold of the Bogwitch myself, when in fact I should have found some good mortal to do it. I had a daughter, thinking that, as the child of a mortal woman, she would be able to take the acorn and wake the Valley Bottom Badger, and defeat the Bogwitch. That was why I sent her into hiding with her mother at Rise Cottage. Gem's mother never forgave me for her death. There was too much of the Badgerman in Gem for her to succeed in her task. The decision to act against the Bogwitch has to come from a human heart. I can see that now. Gem was doomed from the time she left this house.'

Steve was relieved when the Badgerman paused for breath. He felt exhausted, as if he too had lived through the last forty-four years, and had aged as much.

'But unlike me,' the Badgerman went on, 'she has stuck to her purpose. She saw the good in you, Stephen, and now you have come to rouse me from my stupor. The great Badger must be woken. She is a creature of unimaginable power. She may be a force for great good, but if she is roused with evil intent she will reek havoc. She cannot be controlled, but may be influenced. Ramswold is in great need of her now.'

Steve shuddered with foreboding.

'When the Autumn Equinox comes,' said the Badgerman, 'the Bogwitch will be at the height of her power. She'll be in the mill with Gem's silver trinket, trying to raise the

Badger from her sett deep in the Oakridge. And you will have to face her alone.'

The Badgerman leaned across the table and grasped Steve's trembling arm. When he spoke, his voice was calm.

'But between now and then,' he said, 'there is much work to be done.'

16

It was only when Steve fumbled for his radio and couldn't find it that he remembered he was in the back bedroom of Rowan Cottage. It was a small room, dominated by the double bed in which he had slept. The walls had once been painted thrush-egg blue, but now dark stains had spoiled them. Steve rolled over and buried his head under the pillow.

The Badgerman shouted up the stairs. 'Stephen! Stephen! Are you not up yet?'

'Yes,' he called ambiguously.

Steve hauled himself out of bed and put on his clothes. His mouth was parched and his throat as sore as if he'd been trying to swallow autumn leaves.

When Steve entered the kitchen, the Badgerman had already made a pot of tea and was busying himself with the frying pan. A night of uninterrupted sleep had further improved his temper.

'What time is it?' Steve yawned.

'Gone twelve,' said the Badgerman. 'Time for a bath. The bucket's outside the door. Towel's over there. The pump in the yard's good enough for me, so it's good enough for you.'

'If you say so,' said Steve.

'The water comes straight from an underground spring, pure as from All's Well.'

The pump handle was stiff, requiring all Steve's strength to shift it, but once he'd got it moving, a foaming torrent gushed into the bucket and spilled over the sides. When Steve jerked up the handle, the pump shuddered in protest and let out one last gout of water before the flow was finally shut off.

Steve took off his clothes, raised the metal pail above his head and flipped it over him. The icy water hit his head and roared about his ears. In the quiet that followed, his mind cleared of all the tiredness he had felt since the fire. Immediately he refilled the bucket and repeated the process. He no longer felt the cold.

After breakfast, Steve followed the Badgerman back into the yard.

'I put it up there,' said the old man, mysteriously pointing to the storeroom above the kitchen. 'It's about time I got it out again. You'll soon see what the acorn's for, apart from waking the Badger!'

When they reached the top of the narrow steps at the end of the cottage, the Badgerman took an iron key from his shirt pocket and put it in the door. The lock snapped back, but the door refused to open until a mighty kick from the Badgerman sent it crashing against an old Welsh dresser, abandoned in the corner of the room.

The Badgerman felt around for the switch and clicked on the light. The room was a tangle of junk.

'Right, Stephen,' he said, 'grab these and chuck them down into the yard.'

Steve found himself holding a splintered standard lamp in one hand and an old-fashioned cricket trophy in the other. They landed at the foot of the steps with a satisfying crash.

It took them half an hour to reach the back of the workshop, by which time the yard below the steps was piled high with household junk. Still remaining was a wardrobe, behind which were stacked sheets of veneer and a heavy bundle of wooden beading. Beyond them Steve could just see the edge of a circular table, upended against the rear wall.

'Right, let's put some elbow into it then, Stephen,' said the Badgerman, 'and we'll have it out.'

Removing the wardrobe was easy, but the large sheets of veneer were delicate and had to be moved one at a time. When they had stacked them neatly against the side wall they manhandled the table down the steps.

The table top was thick with cobwebs and dust, and if it ever had a set of legs they had long since been discarded. It was only when they had set it down on the kitchen table, and the Badgerman had taken a cloth to it, that Steve saw what they had recovered.

The table had been beautifully carved, and inlaid with woods of many delicate shades, but many of the veneers had begun to crack and some of the inlays were now missing. The table was a vast map – not a map of the world, but a map of the Ramswold Valley, each detail carefully recorded. Rise Cottage was there, so was the Bogwitch's cottage and Bassetts Mill. Every house and every street was plain to see, as a small rectangle or strip of beading, but some details were wrong; this was the map of Ramswold thirty years ago. There were no industrial units, where Monk had his workshop, and the cycle path was still marked as the Mill Bottom Branch Line. The piano factory, too, was there in all its former glory.

'Did you make this?' asked Steve, entranced by the intricate craftsmanship. 'It must have taken ages!'

The Badgerman cast a sad eye over his handiwork. 'Yes, it took a long time, but I've neglected it, just like everything else. Restoring and updating it will keep us both busy well into September.'

Steve ran his hand over the peeling surface. It was still

good to touch, like the font in St Peter's. Pricey would have loved it.

'Did Nathan Sawyer ever see this?' asked Steve.

The Badgerman shook his head. 'I didn't know him well. We met in the woods once or twice. He told me about his idea for the font and I gave him the wood. He never suspected who I really was.'

'And was it really made from the oldest oak?'

'Oh yes, but I hadn't felled it in his lifetime. This table, too, is just one great cross-section of its trunk.'

'And the rest of it?' said Steve.

'Safe,' said the Badgerman, 'but the most important part of it is still in your pocket.'

He held out his hand so Steve could place the acorn in his palm.

'Now, watch!'

The Badgerman tapped the hub of the table where Old Lardy met the Wool Water at the centre of the four woods. A section of map two inches square rotated about its horizontal axis to reveal a small cavity beneath. The Badgerman placed the acorn in the opening and closed the lid.

'There,' he said, 'back at the centre of the world where it belongs!'

'But what's the table for?' asked Steve.

'Eating off, of course. Now make a pot of tea and I'll show you.'

When the tea was made, Steve was at a loss where to set down the mugs.

'Put them on the table,' said the Badgerman, laying two place mats on the edge of Whistlers' Wood. 'Like the world, it's for using, not abusing. Though what right I have to talk, I don't know.'

When Steve had sat down, the Badgerman asked, 'What would you like to see most?'

'Sorry?'

'If you could go anywhere in Ramswold, where would you most like to go?'

'Home.'

'Ah,' said the Badgerman, placing his hands over the small square of veneer which represented Rise Cottage, 'I think that might be difficult. Better choose somewhere else to start with. Move your hand to another place you'd like to go.'

When Steve ran his fingers across the surface of the table, the delicate shades of brown and gold became a blur of green. The sounds of the wind seemed to rush down the chimney and out through the stove into the kitchen.

'Not so fast,' cautioned the Badgerman.

Steve's finger found Pricey's house. His eyes settled on the surface of the table. The veneer fell away and he could see Pricey's front door. Then his hand slipped and he was lost in a green fog. The Badgerman pulled his arm away and the room jumped back into focus.

'It takes practice.'

Steve felt drained, as if he'd run to Ramswold and back without stopping, yet he had never left his seat.

'Did I really?' he began.

'Stand outside your friend's house? In a manner of speaking.'

'It's incredible, and it made me so tired!'

'You're not used to it and the table is in poor condition. We'll improve it.'

'Why didn't you let me see my house? Because it's burnt out?'

'No. Do you have enough strength left to look?' the Badgerman asked, his eyes full of concern.

'I don't know. I'll try anyway.'

'Place your fingers over the exact spot then, don't brush them across the table like you did before.'

Steve did as he was instructed.

'Fog,' he said. 'Nothing but a damp autumn fog. I can't see anything.'

'The Bogwitch. Her influence. You will see it too at Paupers' Pond, but even more impenetrable.'

'And at the Railway Hotel?'

'You're learning.'

'So I won't be able to see my brother Richard?'

'Not while he remains in that house, no.'

'And my mum and dad?'

'We shall have to look for them when the table is in a better state of affairs. At the moment, it is a rather grimy window on the world. You must remain patient.'

'Are they all right, though?'

'I don't know. Even when it is in peak condition the table only allows me a glimpse of what is going on in people's lives. I can look, I can hear the sounds of the wood – the trees, the creatures, the breeze, birds singing – but I cannot hear the human voice. The table is not a means of prying. I can only look and make a guess. It is often best not to look too hard.'

'And what did you see the night Gem died?'

'Nothing,' the Badgerman replied, sadly. 'She had the acorn, remember. She had taken the heart of the table with her. When she didn't return, I stopped maintaining it. There was no point.'

'Why mend it now then, if you mean me to take the acorn too?'

'You must learn about the valley. You must learn how to work in wood. You must help me make the changes to the map. You have the knowledge I need and, by repairing the table, we might yet begin to repair the world.'

'But what use will the table be,' Steve insisted, 'when the acorn is gone?'

'If you do what is required of you,' the Badgerman said, firmly, 'finding another acorn to plant at the heart of the table will not be a problem.'

'But . . .' Steve began.

'No time for that. We must make a start!'

17

So the days passed. Steve rose at seven each morning to find the Badgerman already hard at work checking the changes he had made to the table the previous evening. Steve would cook breakfast, and examine the snares at the bottom of the paddock. When he had collected the eggs and fed the hens, he would put in a couple of hours with the axe. At half-past ten he doused himself with water from the pump, and then went in to make a pot of tea. After that, he would assist the Badgerman for the rest of the day.

On Sundays they took a break. The Badgerman would lead Steve down to the cellar and out through a door at the far end, to explore his network of tunnels. Their excursions ended with a stroll along the passageway that surfaced in the rowan-ringed quarry where the badger clans had met. There they would sit in the sun for an hour or so until the Badgerman deemed it no longer wise to be out. Below them it was just possible to see the chimney of Rowan Cottage and the Wood Spring bridge. It was there, on the second Sunday in September, that Steve saw his friend Pricey leaning over the parapet.

Steve stood up as if to call, but the Badgerman pulled him down.

'It's no good. He wouldn't hear you,' he said, and then cautioned, 'and remember what I said about it being dangerous to make too much noise. We've risked too much already. We must go.'

Seeing Pricey put Steve into a gloomy mood, which the

Badgerman found hard to dispel. Seclusion within the circle of trees at Rowan Cottage was all very well as long as you didn't give much thought to the outside world. The reappearance of Pricey and the completion of the table on the second Thursday in September brought events sharply back into focus. By lunchtime they had cleared up the kitchen. It only remained for Steve to buff up the table with a soft cloth, while the Badgerman prepared a meal and brewed up a pot of tea. By the time Steve had finished polishing it looked as if the world had already been made anew.

'What do you think?' asked the Badgerman.

'Not bad,' said Steve.

'Hmm. Let's not fool ourselves. It's not good either. Not yet. It's just the beginning.'

'Actually, I think it's a wonder!' said Steve.

'Don't let it go to your head. It's only the world as it should be, not as it is. Shall we try it out?'

The Badgerman reached into his shirt pocket and handed the acorn to Steve.

'Put it back where it belongs,' he said. 'The weather's changing. We can stoke up the stove and spend the afternoon at the table.'

Lunch was an unnerving experience. Not because it seemed wrong to eat off such a beautiful creation as the table, but because every time Steve moved his knife and fork, he was overcome by the sensation of rushing breathlessly through Whistler's Wood towards High Force. It was not good for the digestion. The Badgerman, however, allowed his fingers to play over Ramswold as he ate, and remained undisturbed by the experience.

When they had cleared away, the Badgerman said: 'I think there's something you should see. You must take a look at Ramswold.'

The old man's serious tone made Steve wary. He placed his hand on the square which represented Rowan Cottage and found himself looking across the paddock towards the goat. The afternoon had clouded over, but all seemed well behind the screen of rowans. Moving his fingers, he passed from the garden into a world of silence on the main road. Cars moved fast, but without sound. They passed through a veil of mist, but without lights. The mist thickened to fog as he moved across the table towards Paupers' Pond where the world became dark. Beyond the pond, houses here and there stood out stark in the mist. A chill ran up through Steve's fingers as he entered Ramswold. There was Mrs Titmarsh's. The shop window was lit up. Already she was rearranging last year's faded stock, dusting it down in readiness for another Christmas. She looked tidier than usual. It was early closing. Perhaps she would be going out. Steve moved on to Pricey's house. Steve approached the door, reluctant to enter. The Badgerman encouraged him.

'Keep your fingers close together. Hold them steady.'

Pricey was there. So was Monica. They should have been at school, but they were all dressed up, still tanned from their holiday. Pricey looked like he was going to perform at a concert, uncomfortable as ever in starched collar and black tie. Mrs Price too was there, adjusting her hair in the mirror. She too was dressed in black. And Mr Price. Someone had died. They were going to a funeral. Pricey's grandmother?

But when Steve left the house and moved up the High Street to St Peter's he was suddenly confused. There was Mrs Titmarsh again, and she was talking to Pricey's grandmother. Then a blue van pulled up. His father got out of the passenger door. Malcolm Monk emerged from the driver's side and came round to join him on the pavement. They said hello to the two old ladies by the lych gate and

146

went down the path to the church. A few moments later a taxi arrived: his mother and Richard, both dressed in black. Richard had even polished his shoes. He never ever did that. He was quiet. His mother said nothing. But at least they were together. Steve followed them into the church. Everybody was sitting in rows silently facing the front. Half of Ramswold seemed to be there.

The vestry door opened and Pricey made his way to the organ loft. He shuffled on to the stool and began to play. The sound was muted, but plain. The vicar looked pleased with himself and began the service. His father and then Richard went up to give the readings. Their lips moved soundlessly. They were reading for him. He jerked his hand away from the table and sat back in a cold sweat.

'Memorial service,' he mumbled. 'Memorial service for me!' Then he rounded on the Badgerman in fury. 'Why did you make me see? My mum and dad aren't back together even! Why did you let me see?'

'If you stay too long behind the rowans, you become complacent,' said the Badgerman. 'It was time to look.'

'So you knew,' shouted Steve. 'That's what you've been doing early in the mornings before I get up. You've been putting the acorn in and taking a look!'

'What did you expect me to do, Stephen? I'm the Badgerman. It's my job.'

'You could have told me,' said Steve, getting up from the table. 'You could have warned me.'

'I did. You heard it in my voice.'

Steve stood up and pushed his chair away from the table. 'I'm going out to chop wood!'

All that afternoon, while the Badgerman played his fingers across the table, Steve wielded the axe with a vengeance. By the time the rain began to shake the leaves of the rowans, he had calmed down.

'Bogwitch,' he said, 'I mustn't forget the Bogwitch.'

He tried to remember Gem's skipping songs, but he couldn't, only what they had told him to do.

One more event occurred to disturb his routine before the Equinox came. It happened on the day before, the Sunday. The Badgerman had just come in from manuring the vegetable garden and was drying his hands after washing them under the pump. Steve was sitting at the table allowing his well-practised fingers to glide through the fog on the main road. Few places in Ramswold were clear of this evil mist any more. A figure dressed in his Sunday best had just passed the Duck and Enter.

'It's Pricey!' he exclaimed. 'Coming this way, I think. He must have been to church again.'

The Badgerman sat down to have a look. Together they followed his progress to the Wood Spring bridge. He stopped and crossed the road. Then he looked over the parapet. He was staring upstream at what he realized was a line of trees heavy with rowan berries. Steve could almost read his thoughts. Pricey continued on his way, all the while looking up at the trees. He stopped when he came to the green front gate. He opened it and came down the path.

Although Steve had expected it, the proximity and loudness of Pricey's knock made him jump and he lost his connection with the map. The Badgerman was startled also. He got up and pushed Steve down under the table.

'Don't move and don't breathe a word,' he said.

When Pricey knocked again, the Badgerman went out into the hall. By the time he reached the door, their visitor had gone round the house to the back and was rapping urgently on the kitchen window.

'Hang on! Hang on!' shouted the Badgerman as he strode back down the hall. He sounded as angry as on the

148

day Steve had first met him. He flung open the back door with a belligerent flourish.

'Yes?' he said. 'What do you want?'

Pricey was taken aback, but he held his ground. He was desperate. 'I'm looking for Mr Brockworth,' he said.

'Who?'

'Mr John Brockworth. I thought he lived here.'

'Well, he doesn't,' said the Badgerman. 'Now if . . .'

But Pricey had put his foot in the door as the Badgerman had begun to close it.

'I was hoping Mr Brockworth might be able to tell me something about the Badgerman,' Pricey continued, breathlessly. 'We were trying to find him. That is, before my friend died. It's important. The Bogwitch – Mrs Savage – is going to kill someone else tomorrow. This is a photo of my friend. Look. I'm not sure he's really dead. Have you seen him? I think Mrs Savage may have got him or else he's hiding somewhere, but why he hasn't got in touch . . .'

Pricey dribbled to a stop.

Steve wanted to push the table away. Had Pricey noticed its intricacy? Had he spotted it for what it was? Surely the Badgerman would invite him in and tell him that everything was all right, that after tomorrow things would be fine again. But all he said was: 'I don't know what you're talking about! Are you mad? Being rude about the Mayor like that. If you don't leave this minute, I'll call the police!'

Pricey uttered a pathetic sound, half sob, half obscenity, and left to make his miserable way home.

'Why didn't you tell him?' said Steve angrily, when his friend had gone.

'Why didn't you reveal yourself?' snapped the Badgerman. 'I couldn't have stopped you?'

'You told me not to.'

'Do you always do everything people tell you to do?'

'Well, should I have let him know that I was here?'

'And given yourself away to the Bogwitch? It was your choice, not mine.'

'But he came here because he wanted to do something about her.'

'He's brave as well as talented,' said the Badgerman, 'and loyal.'

'Couldn't we have told him? What if he tries to do something crazy tomorrow night? What if he tries to take on the Bogwitch himself? We *should* have said something, if only to stop that.'

The Badgerman turned away and began to riddle the stove.

'It's him!' said Steve, seeing it all. 'It's him she wants, isn't it? The most talented of his generation. She's wanted Pricey all along. And you knew that when he came here. Why did you let him go?'

The Badgerman turned back to face Steve. 'Why didn't you show yourself? Go now, and tell him! Chase after him! The door of Rowan Cottage is not locked.'

Steve got up from his seat, but couldn't leave the room.

'A Badgerman has to make hard decisions,' the old man continued. 'Do you think I want him to fall prey to the Bogwitch? Do you think I'll enjoy sitting here by the stove tomorrow night while you and he are alone in the woods with that creature? Go now and stop him if you want.'

'Will I still be able to save him tomorrow?' said Steve, sitting back down at the table to think.

'I don't know that, Stephen,' said the Badgerman. 'There are many things that I don't know. It will depend on you.'

Steve couldn't sleep that night, and not long after the Badgerman had retired to bed he stole back down to the kitchen. The weather had finally broken. A cold, rising wind buffeted the chimney, the fire roared and sparks shot

150

upwards into the night sky. The windows of the cottage rattled. Rain hammered the trees and hissed in the heart of the stove.

He sat down and laid both hands on the table. High Force roared in his ears as he dived from the platform of rock at the top, deep into the dark water of All's Well and on over the weir towards the mill. The Oakridge stirred under his right hand, its breathing slow and sonorous, while his left hand floated down stream into the inpenetrable darkness of the mill. Was the Bogwitch already there, waiting? He couldn't tell.

The whole valley was locked in a fastness of mist. The deep gloom of Rising Wood was only broken by the shimmering trail of a lame badger. Steve followed it until it disappeared underground. It reappeared some twenty minutes later on the Wood Spring bridge. It crossed the road and snuffled into the garden of Rowan Cottage itself. It had come to eat carrots. Steve left the table and crept down the hall to the front door. When he opened it, the badger raised its head and stared at him unperturbed. Steve called to it through the driving rain, but it wouldn't come to him. It bent its head to take one last carrot and then shuffled off the way it had come. By the time Steve returned to the table it had vanished.

Steve's parents were out of view in Mill Bottom, but he found Pricey still awake. He was sitting at his desk in front of an electronic keyboard. It was plugged into his computer and he had his headphones on. He looked older. He was playing the keyboard with his left hand and tapping the computer keys with the other. There were papers on his desk. He had written a title, Skipping Song for Monica, and then crossed it out. Underneath he had scrawled: *climb the ridge and plant your seed*, and underlined it. Pricey was restless too. Steve could see that he was itching to work it all

off on his saxophone, but didn't dare for fear of bringing the
wrath of the household down upon him. Eventually he tore
off his headphones and threw himself on to the bed. It
would be so easy for Steve to turn up at the house, but it
wouldn't solve anything. He must watch and wait.

Steve was not sure what time he himself drifted off, but
the Badgerman found him asleep at six o'clock, arms
stretched out across the four woods, his head resting on the
table. At the Badgerman's touch Steve woke with a start
from a dream of wolves and wild boar.

'How's Pricey?' said the Badgerman.

'What?' said Steve.

'I said, how's Pricey this morning?'

Steve looked into the table. 'He's still asleep.'

'Good,' said the Badgerman. 'Now, how about breakfast?
Don't disturb yourself, I'll get it. What time does Pricey get
up?'

'As late as possible usually.'

Pricey always ate on the hoof in the morning, and Steve
couldn't help laughing as he watched him dash down the
road: school bag over his shoulder, saxophone case in one
hand, sports kit in the other, two slices of toast flapping
from his clenched teeth. The school bus was pulling away
from the stop by the time he reached it, but it slowed down
for him. The doors hissed open and Pricey hurled himself
aboard. That was the last Steve saw of him until he repeated
the performance in reverse order, chocolate bar now
substituted for toast, late that afternoon.

'You still haven't decided what to do about Pricey?' asked
the Badgerman, coming in from the rain at half-past six to
start the evening meal.

'No,' Steve said.

'If you want to go to him, then that's still your decision.'

'And you won't help me make it?'

'No.'

'How's she going to kill him?'

'I told you, the table can't tell us everything. It could be any time after he enters the fog. As long as you can see him, he'll be OK.'

'But there's fog everywhere,' Steve protested.

'What's he doing now?'

Steve looked. 'Helping his mum make the dinner. He never does that!'

'He's a good lad.'

'No, wait a minute, his mum's leaving the kitchen. Monica wants her to look at something on the TV. He's searching through the drawers. Idiot! Pricey! Can't you see the ladle's stuck, you'll never get it open wrenching it like that.'

The Badgerman came over to see.

At last Pricey got the drawer open, and rummaged through the utensils. Rejecting the palette knife he selected a small stainless steel meat cleaver and a sharp wooden-handled kitchen knife with a four-inch blade. He stuffed them quickly into his back pocket and pulled down his pullover to conceal the handles. Then, adopting an air of innocence, he busied himself with laying the table.

'Does he really know what he's getting into?' Steve asked himself.

'You know him better than I do,' the Badgerman replied.

'Why doesn't he just stay at home? Doesn't he realize?'

'Do you think he'd be any safer?'

Steve pressed his fingers hard into the surface of the table. A clap of thunder shook the Top Wolds to the west, beyond Ramswold.

'I'll have to intercept him. I can't just abandon him!'

'Go then. Take your bike,' said the Badgerman. 'It'll be dark soon. There's no time to use the tunnels.'

18

The Badgerman opened the door and sniffed the air. The rain had turned to fine drizzle. Then he stepped aside so Steve could fetch his bike from the back of the Land Rover. When Steve was comfortable in the saddle, the Badgerman strapped his axe to the crossbar.

'Bring it back intact,' he said, 'it's the only one I've got. You know how to use it?'

Steve looked at the great pile of split logs on the other side of the yard. 'If I don't, then I've been wasting my time!'

'And you've got the acorn?'

Steve patted the right-hand pocket of the heavy leather work jacket the Badgerman had altered to fit him.

'Stay off the road,' warned the Badgerman, 'until you get to Ramswold, and give the Railway Hotel a wide berth. Now go, before you lose Pricey!'

When he reached the edge of Whispering Wood Steve looked back across the paddock. The Badgerman waved once and then retreated indoors to wait alone by the range.

As there was no obvious path through the trees, Steve dismounted and clambered up the hill with the bike over his shoulder. At the top he climbed over the dry-stone wall and rode along the edge of the field, parallel to the trees, until the path veered off sharply to a farm on his left. He dismounted and climbed over the fence into Tumbling Wood. Below him, the valley was submerged in fog.

He set off again, slithering diagonally across the slope

until he skidded to a halt in the dry shade of a towering oak. The ground beneath the tree was strewn with acorns, some brown, but mostly green. He propped his bike up against the trunk and bent down on his hands and knees. The green acorns glowed faintly in the dark, but he rejected these. Instead he ran his hands across the ground, seeking the rarer brown ones which had fallen the previous year. There weren't very many, but enough. He slipped them into his left pocket.

When he reached the recreation ground, he burst out of the wood and pedalled fast across the football pitch. He didn't stop until he reached the junction with the High Street. He looked right, and saw his brother Richard coming up the hill towards him.

There was no time to turn back. At the very least, Richard had recognized the bicycle.

'Hey!' his brother called, and broke into a run.

Steve thought about making a dash for it, but in the end he couldn't bring himself to do it. He free-wheeled down the hill.

'Is it really you?' asked Richard, taking hold of the handlebars to prevent him escaping. He touched Steve's hands. 'Is it really you?'

Steve nodded.

'Pricey said you were still alive,' Richard continued. 'I thought he was crazy. No one else believed him.'

'Did he say anything else?' asked Steve.

'No. He doesn't speak to anyone. He just plays music all the time. But where've you been? Mum and Dad were so upset.'

'Look, I've got to go,' said Steve.

'He had seen Pricey appear at the end of his road, riding his father's bike. He was wearing Monica's pink backpack. Now he was turning right, down the hill.

Steve pressed on the pedals, but Richard held the bike firm.

'What am I supposed to tell Mum and Dad?' he cried.

Steve was distracted for a moment. 'What?' he said. 'Are they back together?'

'No.'

'But you're talking to them?'

'Yes. Since the fire. But they won't talk to each other. What am I supposed to tell them?'

Pricey had gone past the junction at the foot of the hill. Steve hadn't seen which road he had taken.

'I've got to go,' said Steve. 'Look, it's complicated . . . I'll tell you later . . . now I really must go!'

Richard relented and stepped aside.

'Where are you going?' he shouted, as Steve sped off.

But he got no reply.

Steve understood his friend well enough to know that he wouldn't be sure what he intended to do. Pricey would probably just wait for the Bogwitch outside her house on the main road.

That is, if he made it that far.

By the time Steve reached the foot of the hill he was in fifteenth gear. Riding without lights, he sped into the icy fog which blanketed the road between Ramswold and Little Dipping, but before long he had to brake hard as he came up fast behind a van at the end of a queue of traffic.

Drizzle hung in the air as freezing droplets. Windscreen wipers laboured back and forth. The valley was full of the Bogwitch's cruel breath. Steve swung the bike up on to the pavement. Where was Pricey? Horns were blaring. A dog barked. At the head of the queue people seemed to be frozen in their cars.

A tree was down thirty yards from the Duck and Enter. It was a tall ash. He could see its black outline against the fairy

156

lights of the pub. The upper branches had splintered about the bus shelter. Five figures had formed a semi-circle close to the fallen tree.

'Pricey!' Steve shouted. Then as he accelerated towards the gathering, he called: 'Adam Hoggis, get your hands off!'

The fat boy whirled round. Then the fog closed about the gang, hiding them, but Steve kept the bike steady. He hit the outer branches sooner than he anticipated, but he held on to the handlebars as his body lurched forwards and twisted sideways.

Shapes moved in and out of the fog, searching for him. Branches snapped and shattered. Distantly a fire engine wailed, but it seemed to be in another valley. Steve tore the axe from the crossbar and, as he slashed at the clawing wood, he shouted the names of the gang one after another, starting with Gem. Not one of them dared come near as he demolished the top of the tree.

The fog began to thin and the gang retreated into Whistlers' Wood. Voices became audible on the main road. Steve hacked through the last branch blocking the entrance to the shelter and heaved it aside.

Pricey was in the corner, cowering behind his bike.

He stared at Steve in horror. The concrete roof of the bus shelter had saved him for what? To meet a more terrifying death at the end of an axe? He screamed, but Steve clamped his hand over his mouth to silence him.

'Shut up, Pricey!' he said. 'It's me. We've got to get out of here quick. The last thing we want is to be carted off to hospital in an ambulance!'

Pricey was too stunned to argue. Steve pulled him up, and together they manoeuvred the foldaway bike out of the tangle of branches. A chorus of shouts went up, but they didn't stop to wait for the yellow-helmeted men who had appeared on the edge of the fog. Instead, they retrieved

157

Steve's mountain bike and fled the same way as Savage's gang, up the slope into Whistlers' Wood.

'Where are we going?' Pricey asked, when they had stopped to catch their breath some quarter of a mile from the road. He wanted to ask other questions, but there was no time.

'As far from falling trees as possible,' said Steve.

'Better get a move on then,' laughed Pricey, looking up at the great ash which disappeared into the fog above them. 'There's no bus service through here!'

'There is at Little Dipping though, not that you're going to catch one. You're going to have to stay put at St Thomas's.'

'Why?'

'Shhh. Listen!'

'To what?'

Pricey couldn't hear anything.

'She's called the gang back. The dogs are in the wood. She's regrouping. In the meantime, she still means to get you!'

'And you, too?'

'Yes, but you'll be safe in the church. If she can't get you, then she'll be weakened.'

'And if she kills you?'

'At least you'll be able to visit my grave, not like last time.'

'I played at your memorial though,' Pricey protested.

'I know,' said Steve, 'I saw you.'

'Where were you, Steve? Why didn't you get in touch? You found the Badgerman, didn't you? You could have come and told me!'

'I'll tell you about it later,' said Steve. 'The Bogwitch would just love us to fall out. She'll concentrate on defending the mill. You know about the Valley Bottom Badger?'

158

'I think so,' said Pricey. 'Asleep under the Oakridge?'

'Now that the Bogwitch knows I'm alive, she'll be working harder than ever to wake her. That gives us a chance to get you to St Thomas's. Get your knife and cleaver out now.'

'How do you know about them?'

'The Badgerman,' Steve began, then broke off. 'Listen!'

Pricey couldn't hear anything.

'Quick, put your bike down,' hissed Steve. 'Give me the knife. One of the dogs is between us and the church. The others are spreading out.'

Steve cut the straps from Monica's bag. Lowering his voice, he whispered urgently: 'Stand with your back to that tree. Don't move.'

Then he chopped down an ash pole, trimmed off the branches, and used the straps to lash the knife to the end. When he'd checked the binding, he gave it to Pricey.

'Hold your ground,' he instructed. 'Keep the cleaver handy in your belt.'

Pricey made some tentative forward thrusts. Steve turned his attention to his mountain bike. Swiftly, he removed the wheels and snapped off the chain with a sharp blow of the axe. Then, when he had stowed them by the tree, he buried the axe in the trunk above his head, for safe-keeping. Finally, he took up his position with his back to Pricey.

'What about the Bogwitch and the others?' whispered Pricey. 'What if they come here after all?'

'They won't,' said Steve. 'Just concentrate on holding the dogs off. I'll do the rest.'

The first dog appeared to Pricey's right, its shoulders down, teeth bared. A second appeared further down the slope. Pricey was their target.

'Keep your eye on the dog to your right!' shouted Steve. 'And get that knife up!'

159

But he was wasting his breath. Pricey was mesmerized and couldn't respond. Steve reached for the front wheel of his bike and hurled it at the furthest of the two dogs. The wheel bounced short and catapulted off a tree. The dog flinched just long enough for him to aim the second. It caught the Dobermann on the rump, knocking him off balance, and then rolled harmlessly away. The other dog closed on Pricey but, instead of leaping at his throat, tore at the end of his makeshift spear, dragging him away from the tree. As it towed Pricey round in an effort to bring him down, Steve picked up the frame of the mountain bike, and heaved it into the path of the other dog. The front forks hit the ground just as the dog took off. The bottom bracket bounced upwards, ramming the chain wheel into the dog's chest. The Dobermann toppled forward and rolled over on to its back – one front paw flapping uselessly – as it struggled to free itself from the bicycle frame.

Pricey stumbled and let go of the ash pole.

'Cleaver!' shouted Steve, but there was no time for Pricey to do anything but curl up into a tight ball as the dog tore at him. Before Steve could respond, the third Dobermann hurtled out of the fog, bundling him back against the tree as its front feet hammered into his chest.

As he hit the ground, with the full weight of the mad dog on top of him, he reached out for the bicycle chain. But before he could find it, a second, more powerful animal was upon him. For a moment his mouth was full of stinking fur. Claws raked across his body as the old boar badger locked its jaws round the Dobermann's neck and began to thrash it against the tree. Then Steve was free. He grabbed the bicycle chain and struggled to his feet.

Disoriented for a moment, he looked around. The second dog had freed itself from the bicycle frame and was limping away into the fog. Pricey lay still, his head bloody.

His attacker straddled him, uncertain whether to flee after his companion or finish the job. Steve flung himself at the dog and slipped the bicycle chain round its neck like a choker and jerked it clear of Pricey. It came to heel, eyes bulging, gasping for breath. Pricey grunted and rolled over on to his back. The badger from Rising Wood raised its head from the other Dobermann, which lay dead at the foot of the tree, and looked at them.

'You all right, Pricey?' said Steve.

Pricey rubbed his hand across his mouth and sat up. His voice trembled at the sight of blood on his fingers.

'Think so,' he said, 'I'm just glad I wore two pullovers, that's all!'

Pricey noticed the badger for the first time. It had settled down by its kill, and was nuzzling the earth.

'Blimey,' he said, 'where did he come from?'

Steve didn't answer. Instead, he asked his own question: 'Shall I put this one out of its misery?'

When he tightened the chain, the dog lay down on its side to acknowledge Steve's superiority.

'Doesn't look so dangerous when he does that,' said Pricey, getting to his feet. 'Looks like an ordinary mutt. I feel a bit sorry for it. Are you going to let the badger have it then, or let it go?'

Pricey couldn't kill it any more than Steve could.

As if sensing as much, the old boar badger sniffed the corpse of his victim one last time, and then shuffled off in the direction of High Force.

'It's time we moved,' said Steve, 'we'll have to take the dog with us.'

19

When they reached the wall of St Thomas's churchyard the dog dug its claws into the earth and refused to be led any further.

'Pity that badger didn't just kill it,' said Pricey irritably, forgetting for a moment that he was lucky to be alive.

'Stop moaning,' said Steve, 'and shove your dad's bike over the wall.'

Pricey did as he was told and then clambered over himself.

'You next,' said Steve, hauling the dog over the wall. They left the Dobermann by Adam Hoggis's tombstone, chained to the rusty wheelbarrow.

When they reached the church door, Steve said, 'You'll be safe as long as you stay up the tower.'

'But how do we get in?' said Pricey. 'I thought this place was locked.'

'It is,' said Steve, 'so you'd better pray the vicar's deaf! Stand back so I can get a good swing at this thing.'

With a well-timed blow of the axe, the lock snapped and the door swung open.

'There! Now get up the tower, quick. Bolt the door at the top and bottom. When the fog clears, keep your eye on the Oakridge. If you don't see anything tonight, don't come down until tomorrow morning. If you don't see me again, try to explain it all to Richard, OK?'

Before Pricey could say anything, Steve shoved him through the door and raced off towards Old Lardy, and the top of Whistlers' Wood.

Steve ran across the fields for about a mile until he came to the stream above High Force.

As he stepped into the shelter of the trees, the old boar badger burst out of the underbrush and without a backward glance raced off ahead of him. Steve followed. After twenty yards the badger turned right and, for a moment, he lost it among the trees.

Steve stopped and listened. Rain spattered in the upper branches. Then there was a scuffling and he saw the badger chasing its tail in a frenzy. Then it disappeared into nothing.

There was an opening in the ground. The entrance was no more than two feet wide and eighteen inches high. Steve shoved his axe into the hole and squirmed in after it, feet first. The tunnel was tight as a drainage pipe for ten feet, then it broadened out and fell steeply away into the depths of the earth. He could smell the badger ahead of him. It slowed, waiting for him to gain ground. Only when it was sure that Steve sensed the way did it shoot off ahead.

Eventually Steve was able to stand up, although at a crouch, and began to navigate the tunnel with increasing confidence. Distance was hard to gauge, but he knew from the strain on his ankles that he was travelling deep into the hill. Then, quite suddenly, the badger doubled back and shot past his legs in a pungent rush of heat and fur, leaving him in a quandary.

He stopped to listen, and tightened his grip on the axe. The air cooled. The badger's scrabbling died away as it gained the upper reaches of the tunnel. Steve moved cautiously forward again, his head brushing the roof of the passage, until he heard the first faint sound of water slipping ceaselessly through the air. He relaxed his grip and sat down in the dark to rest. The badger from Rising Wood was afraid of the torrent, but he knew it would be his protector and friend.

When the tunnel eventually opened out, it was on to a ledge behind the white wall of water some twenty feet above the Cauldron. Steve allowed his eyes a few minutes to adjust to the water's radiance, and then made the uneasy sideways descent to the edge of the pool. From there he stepped out on to the rocky weir and slipped down into the stream on the other side, thigh-deep in water. The current propelled him forward, and he had to bounce with it to keep his balance until he reached the shallower water where the stream broadened. Rain spattered off his jacket. His hands were numb and his hair was flattened against his skull. But the fog which had stifled the valley for so long had begun to lift. The Bogwitch was concentrating her powers beneath the Oakridge.

Closer to the mill, the stream narrowed. The current quickened about Steve's legs, chilling his calves. His feet began to slip forwards on the flat stones of the stream bed. He stopped for a moment and anchored himself with the axe. The mill rose before him, its roof glistening against the dark hump of the Oakridge. Standing at the end of the mule track were two figures. One was sharpening a stick with a knife and the other was smoking. They were looking down the spur towards Ramswold. Neither seemed particularly determined.

Then a window shattered on the second floor of the mill and Savage bellowed an order. Startled, the two dead boys cursed. Smoky pinched out his cigarette and Saw flung his stick into the stream. They began to patrol the bank in opposite directions. Steve slipped feet first into the current and allowed himself to be sucked down into the mill race.

The noise in the cavity was awesome as the turbulent water swirled under the blades of the wheel and whiplashed back off the stonework. The huge rusted wheel ground round angrily on its shaft. Then it stuck and juddered. A cold draught funnelled into the cavity, bringing with it a faint echo of thunder from the west.

Above Steve's head, there was an open gallery, housing the drive shaft and transmission gear which provided power for the mill. When his eyes had adjusted to the dark, he threw the axe up on to the gallery floor and then squirmed into the space between the wheel and the wall. As he climbed, the wheel grunted menacingly and shifted, threatening to crush him. He pressed himself tighter into the wall and took shallow breaths.

By the time he reached the gallery, his hands were senseless with cold. He rested for a moment, trying to hear the sounds of the mill; there was nothing but the mind-numbing surge of water. Climbing the iron staircase to the floor above, he found himself in a weaving shop. It was empty. He crouched down behind an iron pillar to wait and watch. There was another entrance at the other end of the room. At some time in the past, the metal door had been pulled off its hinges and propped up against the wall.

A sudden movement caused Steve to cling closer to the pillar. Someone had appeared in the doorway. It was the fat boy, Splodge. He grunted and sat down in the workshop with his back to the wall. He pulled off his balaclava and took something from his pocket. He began to eat hungrily. It was a toffee he'd found in the street. The fat boy had sneaked off to eat undisturbed.

'Adam Hoggis!' Steve whispered, just loudly enough for him to hear, but not so clearly that he could be sure that it wasn't just the sound of the water.

The fat boy stood up and looked around guiltily.

'Is that you, Saw?' he hissed, moving further into the room, so that no one could surprise him through the door.

'Over here, Adam Hoggis!' Steve whispered, more loudly this time. He stood up and ran to the next pillar to give the fat boy a glimpse of scurrying shadow.

Adam Hoggis stopped. He chewed nervously and then swallowed hard.

Steve felt sorry for him. 'Adam Hoggis!' he repeated for the third time.

The fat boy cocked his head to one side and shuffled in Steve's direction, a few steps at a time, beginning to sense that he might be offered something. But he was suspicious and was prepared to flee if he had to.

As he came close to the pillar, Steve stepped into view with the axe raised above his shoulder. Startled, Adam Hoggis tripped backwards, and fell heavily on to the floor. Steve said nothing, and made a show of making ready with the axe.

'Please,' spluttered Splodge, wriggling away, 'please don't hit me.'

'Where are the others?' said Steve sharply.

'In the forge at the other end,' gulped the fat boy, 'guarding the Bogwitch. And two in the yard.'

'What's she doing?'

Under threat of the axe, the fat boy showed no reluctance to talk.

'Trying to work the acorn. The Badgerman's acorn, but nothing happens. We thought it was the right one to wake the Badger, but now we don't. She was getting dangerous, so I sneaked off.'

Steve lowered the axe and adopted a less threatening posture. He couldn't find it in his heart to dislike Adam Hoggis. Nevertheless, he didn't trust him.

'I'm not going to hit you,' he said at last.

'Adam Hoggis propped himself up on one elbow. A hint of a smile appeared in his eyes.

166

'It's not you I'm after,' Steve continued. 'It's not your fault.'

'I hate her!' said Adam Hoggis.

Steve allowed him to sit up. Then he asked the fat boy the question which bothered him most.

'Can I trust what you say?'

'Well, I'll tell you something and then you'll trust me,' said Adam Hoggis. 'The Bogwitch is scared of you. Ever since she first saw you, and worse since she discovered you were still alive. She fears you like you was the Badgerman. She says she's going to bury you deep in history, so nobody can ever find you again. And she's going to do the same with everybody else who knows you.'

'And how's she going to do that?' Steve laughed.

'With that acorn of course,' said Adam Hoggis, irritably, thinking that he was being deliberately needled. 'And there's nothing funny about that!'

The fat boy was right. He extended the handle of the axe to Adam Hoggis and pulled him to his feet.

'Show me where they are, then,' he said.

'We must go quietly,' said the fat boy, shakily putting one foot in front of the other.

When they entered the darkness inside the hill, Adam Hoggis took the axe head in his hand and cautiously led the way forward, while Steve kept an unrelenting grip on the handle. The draught from the doorway ahead brought the faintest scent of smoke. It had a familiar smell. He had breathed it before, on the cycle path earlier in the summer. A voice called through the darkness: 'Steve?'

It wasn't Adam Hoggis who had spoken.

'Steve?'

The question was repeated a third time, from somewhere behind them. The tone was familiar, so was the voice. It was Richard. What was he doing here? Steve looked round. For

167

a moment Richard was framed in the doorway, and then he was gone.

Steve made a move to follow, but Adam Hoggis tugged on the axe.

'Steve?' Richard called from the stairwell beyond the door. 'Pricey found me. He couldn't stay up the tower. Mum and Dad are outside.'

Steve had to go to him. He tried to shake the fat boy off.

'Trick,' hissed Adam Hoggis.

'What?' said Steve irritably. He wanted to listen to what Richard had to say.

'Trick!' repeated Adam Hoggis, as if speaking was taking a great effort. 'The Bogwitch knows you're in the mill.'

Steve shrugged him off and rushed for the door, but he didn't get far. The hard flat edge of the axe struck him between his shoulder blades and bounced off the Badgerman's jacket, knocking the wind out of him. He went down on to his knees. Then the fat boy pounced on him, throwing him over on to his back, pinning his arms and breathing toffee into his face. Steve wanted to be sick.

'There's holes in the floor up there,' hissed the fat boy. 'If you go upstairs, you'll fall through and be buried deep in time. Do you want that?'

'What?' said Steve, shaking his head.

'Was a trick,' the fat boy explained wheezily. 'She knows you're here.'

He rolled off and pulled Steve up. The voice called once again and disappeared into the upper regions of the mill.

'Trust me?' asked Adam Hoggis.

'Yes,' he said. He was angry at his own foolishness. Adam Hoggis handed him the axe. 'How did you know you wouldn't kill me when you threw it?'

'I didn't, but what else could I do? I can't run as fast as you.'

'The Bogwitch won't be pleased,' said Steve.

'She never is, but I've got nothing left to lose.'

Steve wasn't so sure about that. There were noises on the floor above. Footsteps moved rapidly over their heads and faded into the heart of the mill.

'Smoky and Saw,' whispered Adam Hoggis. 'They'll be in trouble for letting you in. She'll whip them stupid.'

'How far now?' Steve asked.

'Beyond the next room.'

Steve led the way into the neighbouring workshop. Dimly lit by a crack of light from the distant glow of the forge, it was less dark than the one they had just left. But the smell of smoke was stronger. It made Steve feel light-headed.

'Put this on,' said Adam Hoggis, pulling his balaclava from his pocket.

Steve took it gratefully. It made breathing difficult. Each gasp became like the last, but it filtered out the smoke. Adam Hoggis urged him forward. The door at the far end swung open. An orange light danced through to greet them, then flared up yellow as the Bogwitch ordered Henry Gray to heap more wood on to the fire. Saw and Sniper waited on either side of the door. And Savage stood beyond them with a length of timber in her hand. The Dobermann which had fled from the wood lay dead at her feet.

The Bogwitch was standing amidst a great pile of rubble. Behind her, a hole had been opened up into the side of the hill. She eyed Steve and Adam Hoggis from beneath her crumbling make-up. Her face was streaked with mascara. Perspiration had cut canals in her foundation. The forge burned hot all around her. All her efforts with the acorn had been useless and now she understood that the pendant was nothing but a Badgerman's trick to buy time. She was beside herself with rage. Killing the dog had not been enough.

169

Thunder rumbled down the chimney from overhead.

'Take them!' screamed the Bogwitch.

Steve pushed Adam Hoggis aside and raised his axe. The Bogwitch flinched when she recognized the blade.

'Nathan Sawyer!' Steve shouted, but he might as well have called from inside a tomb.

Then Adam Hoggis spoke up. 'He says, *Nathan Sawyer!*'

Saw hesitated.

Steve tore off the balaclava. His head swam. He lowered the axe.

'Nathan, I was baptized in your font,' he said.

The Bogwitch, who had stepped forward when she saw Steve weaken, backed off.

Adam Hoggis steadied Steve, and pressed the balaclava into his face.

'Listen to him,' he said.

Saw was uncertain. Sniper could barely raise his gun. The memory of past lashes burned into his shoulder. They shuffled aside just enough to let Steve and Adam Hoggis push their way into the room.

But the Bogwitch had recovered and taken a firm grip on Savage's neck.

Once again, Steve removed the balaclava, just long enough to speak: 'Listen, Nathan,' he said, 'we were all christened in your font. Jack Brockworth, the Badgerman, chose yours, remember?'

The expression in Nathan Sawyer's eyes began to soften, and Sniper cried: 'Savage, what should we do?'

Savage began to writhe, trying to free herself from the Bogwitch's grasp.

'Smoky,' shouted Adam Hoggis, 'close the furnace door!'

'Leave it!' screamed the Bogwitch.

But Henry Gray slammed it shut and jumped away. He skirted the room and joined Thomas Smith and Nathan

Sawyer by the door. The smoke began to clear, and Steve threw off his balaclava.

'He's our friend,' shouted Adam Hoggis. 'Help us, Savage.'

As Adam Hoggis spoke, the Bogwitch raked her nails across Savage's head and down her back. The balaclava and rags fell away. Jemima Black stood, dressed as she had been on the day she died. She looked at Steve and smiled, recognition lighting up her eyes.

For a moment Steve and the four dead boys were disarmed, allowing the Bogwitch to tighten her grip on Gem and open the furnace door. The room flared up yellow, infused with green. The Bogwitch dragged Gem towards the flames.

'I've got what you really want!' screamed Steve. 'I'll give it to you if . . .' But the smoke was almost too much.

Steve recovered himself and measured the distance between himself and the Bogwitch, and the probability of striking a clean blow. In turn, the Bogwitch tried to gauge his skill with the axe. She wasn't prepared to risk a wrong guess, and stopped short of casting Gem into the furnace. But she maintained her grip on the Badgerman's daughter and dug her nails into her flesh.

'Close the door!' said Adam Hoggis.

Steve nodded that this was also his wish. The Bogwitch bridled, but did as instructed.

'Give it to me then!' ordered the Bogwitch hoarsely, eyeing Steve's pockets.

'Don't, Steve!' Gem screeched. It was a convincing act.

He set the axe down between his knees and put his right hand into his pocket. He withdrew the ancient acorn and held it up between his finger and thumb.

The Bogwitch released her grip on Gem and moved forward. Gem stepped out of her way. The Bogwitch made a snatch for the acorn, but Steve palmed it with his left hand and quickly raised the axe with his right. The Bogwitch drew back, her eyes fixed on the blade.

The dead boys pressed in close, lest he should need them. Gem worked her way round to join them.

'You can have the acorn,' Steve continued, 'if you release your hold on these four and let them go with Gem.'

'You can't,' pleaded Gem, continuing her charade. 'That's not what I came to you for! It's not what my father wants.'

Adam Hoggis stepped between Gem and Steve in case she launched an attack. The others closed ranks, forcing Gem away. The Bogwitch laughed and reached out a wrinkled hand as a gesture of agreement. Her eyes were hungry.

'Let's see,' she said gesturing with her claw.

'Free the others,' he said.

The Bogwitch waved her arm in a scornful gesture of goodbye, and the rags fell from the dead boys. They exchanged startled glances.

'Trust me, Gem,' said Steve. 'While there's still time, take them to Rowan Cottage. Your father might be able to help.'

'I understand,' she said, and urged her companions through the door.

Only when he was sure that they were gone, did Steve withdraw his hand from his pocket and show the acorn again. He began to back slowly towards the door of the forge, drawing the Bogwitch away from the furnace door. As he stepped over the threshold he raised his hand to wipe the perspiration from his lips. When he returned it to his pocket, the Badgerman's acorn was safely in his mouth.

'Give it me!' screamed the Bogwitch.

Steve took his hand out of his pocket, his fist full of

172

acorns from Tumbling Wood. With a flick of the wrist he scattered them on to the floor. The Bogwitch fell to her knees, desperate to find the right one.

Steve measured a straight line into the dark, and sprinted through the two adjacent workshops until he came to the stairwell. By clawing at the wall with his free hand he wound his way upwards.

By the time he reached the second landing, the Bogwitch was cursing at the foot of the stairs. He sent more acorns scudding down the steps, but to no avail. She ignored them. By the time Steve burst on to the top floor, where at last there were windows, the Badgerman's acorn had grown soft in his mouth. There was no time to remove it. The Bogwitch was looming out of the stairwell a few paces behind. In his panic, Steve gulped in a great lung full of air. To his horror, the acorn was sucked down his throat. Unable to think of anything else to do, he threw down the remaining acorns, and shouted:

'I haven't got any more!'

The Bogwitch faltered, and Steve was able to reach the window at the far end of the workshop where the mill backed on to the Oakridge. The Badgerman's axe made short work of the mouldering window frame, and he scrambled out on to the Oakridge's crumbling scree. The wind was sweet and cool on his face. The clouds above were heavy with rain. Far below him he could see the light glowing in the kitchen of Rowan Cottage. To the west, he could just make out the tower of St Thomas's.

He clambered on up the slope, scrabbling and slipping, gaining ground and then sliding back. But with the aid of the axe he managed to reach the top.

Before he could regain his breath, the heavens opened and the valley was blotted out. Water cascaded down the slope and rushed about the Bogwitch. But onwards she

173

came, desperate for the acorn that he had so foolishly swallowed. Steve knew that it was inevitable that she would reach him. What was he to do when she did? With no other course open to him, he raised the axe above his head. If he could no longer wake the Valley Bottom Badger, he could at least deliver a blow that the Bogwitch would never forget.

Then, as the Bogwitch's hand grappled for his ankles, lightning bit into the blade of the Badgerman's axe and flashed down the shaft, scorching across Steve's back. His body stretched and then stiffened. His feet convulsed and shot downwards into the rock, propelling the Bogwitch before them. He grew sinewy and at the same time felt his body thrust upwards. His heart pounded in a dark fastness of calm. His feet, he understood, were no longer what they were. Ever downwards they went into the rock and as they forked and spread outwards, he knew that an oak had grown within him and around him. He reached out across the sky and caught up the rain in his shuddering branches.

At last, his questing roots touched something sinuous and irascible deep underground. It stirred and settled, then stirred again in a great uproar of rock and falling masonry. The Oakridge shook. Lightning struck for the second time. The mighty tree which had risen on the escarpment fell and burst asunder. Steve stood with his axe amongst the shattered fragments of timber and saw that the mill had been reduced to rubble. The rain stopped. The thunder diminished as the clouds rolled away over the Vale. The night sky cleared. The Bogwitch was gone.

The Valley Bottom Badger lumbered off into the valley, huge and untameable, a vast spectre of rippling fur and muscle dwarfing the landscape. Then by degrees she began to fade and became nothing more than vapour threading through the trees. Steve leant on his axe and stared out into the darkness. Had Pricey seen? Had his family?

174

There was activity down at Rowan Cottage. The engine of the Land Rover turned over, died, and then fired a second time. It pulled out of the drive and disappeared in the direction of Mill Bottom. He wondered if he would ever see the old man again.

Steve bent down and searched through the shattered timber until he found what he was looking for. The acorn was smooth and green, wedged firmly in its cup. He held it up to his face. When he was sure it was the one, he slipped it into his pocket and set off along the ridge.

When Steve reached Rowan Cottage, he found the back door ajar. The kitchen light was on. The stove was lit and the kettle was just coming to the boil. He set his axe down behind the door and picked up the note which had been left against an unopened demijohn of elderflower wine at the centre of the table.

It said:

If you need me, you know where to find me.
The wine is for your mother and father.

JB.

Steve smiled, but he couldn't dwell on the note for long because he had to rush to the stove to stop the kettle boiling over. Before he made himself a pot of tea, he returned to the table and placed his new acorn in the cavity at the centre. Then he sat down and let his hands play over the surface of the great map.

There was Pricey, still up the tower of St Thomas's, waving his arms about and singing. Steve couldn't hear the words, but he knew that at long last Pricey had invented his skipping song for Monica.

But his other hand had already touched Ramswold. The town was ablaze with light. People had turned out of their houses and were still pointing at the sky. The streets shone with rain and water rushed down the gutters. Steve found himself drawn towards Pricey's house. Monica was leaning out of her bedroom window. Mrs Price was trying to get her back to bed, but Monica was having none of it. Monica was pointing down the road. Three figures were approaching the house. Richard was in front. He turned to urge his father and mother to hurry up. It was apparent that they were still not talking to each other, but they were both anxious to find out if Pricey had further news of Steve. What on earth was he going to tell them?

'We'll think of something,' said a voice behind him.

Steve whirled round. 'Gem!' he exclaimed. 'I thought you'd all gone.'

'You still have a lot to learn,' she said. 'But there'll be plenty of time.'

'Where are the others?' Steve asked.

Gem sat down opposite him, and ran her fingers over the fine beading at the edge of the table. She was sad and, for a moment, wouldn't look at Steve.

'They've gone with my father,' she said. 'Don't worry. They'll be all right.'

'And us, will we be all right too?'

'That's up to you,' she said. 'You'll have to go to your family soon. Ramswold will manage without you for a few years yet, but when Pricey has grown up and moved away you must come back to Rowan Cottage.'

'But what about you?'

Gem smiled. 'The acorn will be safe with me,' she said.

'And will I see you again, between now and then?' asked Steve. 'I've hardly had a chance to get to know you.'

'Haven't you?' said Gem. 'Then you will.'